SEED MONEY

B. E. BAKER

Purple
Puppy
Publishing

For Emmy

You are the best cheerleader

always

SEREN

Not all moments in life are created equal.

There's that moment when you're standing on the dance floor and all eyes are on you—your makeup is perfect, your heart is pounding, and you fit into the dress that hung in your closet for six months waiting for you to lose that last ten pounds.

You command the attention of everyone in the room.

All the girls hate you.

All the boys want you.

And maybe a few of the boys hate you and a few of the girls want you, but you get the point.

That moment is not at all the same as the moments you spend lying in bed, your covers up to your chin, binge-watching every season of *Grey's Anatomy* for the third time, a half-eaten container of Ben and Jerry's melting on your nightstand.

Unfortunately, the moment in which I met Fancy Guy was *not* a dance-floor moment. It was more of a binge-watching-*Grey's* kind of moment. The kind of moment that stretches out and drapes itself over everything rudely. The kind of moment you wish could last forever without anyone discovering it existed.

That's when Fancy Guy came into my life.

In other words, it was a Low Point. In my defense, things for me had not been going well. I should have dusted myself off and ended the pity party, but in those long, never-ending moments, you know what you need, but you don't know how to get there. Otherwise, you *would* get there.

Duh.

But that's why I was wearing an old t-shirt of Will's and boxers with Transformers on them, and that's why my hair was rucked up in the back, and that's why I had a Cheerio stuck to my cheek the first time Fancy Guy ever set eyes on me.

We weren't off to the best start.

Actually, he must have thought I was insane.

He wasn't entirely wrong.

DAVE

The first week of second grade, I found a broken digital camera in a box of discarded junk when I went with Dad to the dump. Mom and Dad never cared what we did with garbage as long as it didn't smell, so I stuck it in my pocket. While I was supposed to be doing research for a history paper at school, I googled how to fix cameras that turn on and then shut right back off again. I found a blog post that explained what was wrong.

Once I got home, it only took me twenty minutes to fix it.

I've been jonesing for that same feeling ever since. Taking something that was discarded and fixing it up so that people can use it is the best kind of high. There are very few joys in the world like turning garbage into treasure.

Since then, I've repaired bikes, televisions, and shoes. I've replaced buckles on purses and made them look brand new. . .or close, anyway. I learned to patch tires until they work like new ones, although the guy at the tire shop fired me after three weeks for selling too many used tires. Apparently the new ones have a higher profit margin. People throw away a lot of things in this world that could be saved, if there weren't economic reasons to trash them.

I suppose I shouldn't have been surprised when my friends started calling me 'garbage guy.' But when the people who disliked me picked it up, it became something I couldn't get rid of, not even in high school or college.

It didn't help that my Dad bought a landfill.

His entire family always found it absolutely hilarious that, with the last name of Fansee, he ran a landfill. But early this year, the city bought the land—for an obscene amount—and now he's relocated his business to somewhere far cheaper. The upshot for me is that, after a decade and a half of being mocked for a combination of my own proclivities, my surname, and my dad's occupation, I finally have a plan.

Because Dad split the profits above the cost of his new landfill between my sister and me.

I decided to use my share of the after-tax windfall —all two point five million of it—to start a new business. My one criterion was that it had to have nothing to do with trash. After a lot of poking around, a few online tests, and some chats with friends, I decided to invest in an inn. Since I live in Scarsdale, New York, real estate isn't cheap, but it's a solid investment. Even if my plans go south, I can probably sell whatever I buy and get most of my money back. I'm looking for a property that can earn me a decent income that will also appreciate over time, like my dad's landfill. . .only less embarrassing.

I've spent the entire morning with my high school pal, checking out small inns that are in various stages of disrepair. My brain processes numbers easily, but I'm still struggling because of the number of properties we've seen. "Are we almost done? Because I can't remember if the one with the broken windows was near the bank, or whether that was the one with the dead frog."

Bernie looks up at the sky as if begging for patience. "The one with the dead frog? Really? That hotel had marble floors, a totally refurbished kitchen, and it was within walking distance of the train station."

"Sure, sure," I say. "Remind me why it wasn't a slam dunk?"

"It has that pending lawsuit, and it's only twenty rooms, which makes it a real risk for the price."

It's been three days of nonstop appointments. I thought it would be *fun* searching for the perfect inn. But the big difference between hotels and inns, I've discovered, is that hotels are generally larger, and inns are often independently owned. Also, they capitalize on being *unique*. Only, none of the places we've seen really stood out as unique to me. Actually, they were all so similar that I'm left identifying them by their location and the dead critters we saw inside.

"What about that one with the lizard skeleton dangling from the office window?" That one was a screaming deal, for somewhat obvious reasons, but neglect I can handle. In fact, it's sort of in my wheelhouse. My budget is quite modest for an inn around this area, and that means my best bet is to find a fixer upper.

"I called on it," Bernie says. "It's under contract."

I sigh. "You still think. . ."

"That you're going to need a partner?" My old

5

friend snorts. "Of course I do. I did mention that I'd be happy to invest."

I could save paying him his cut if he was a partner, which would be nice, but he's also got quite a bit of money saved. The problem is that Bernie's pushy to the point of being almost overbearing. It annoyed me with school projects. I feel like we might kill each other if we went in together on a business deal.

"Or if not me, you know that—"

"Don't say Bentley," I say.

I already know he's thinking it. Bernie, Bentley, and I have been best friends since kindergarten. I had the only normal name, Dave. And our teacher called us 'two Bs and a D.' She thought it was clever. By first grade, the teacher was calling us the three peas in a pod.

They were right about one thing. We were always together.

We still talk all the time and hang out regularly, but as hard as it would be to partner with Bernie, I'm pretty sure Bentley would be even worse. He was always the one of us with loads of money, and that gap has only widened with time. I mean, his name kind of says it all. No normal parents would name their kid *Bentley*. He's old money, he's an intellectual, and he's also stupidly muscular. The only reason I can handle him at all is that he's also a genuinely kind person.

Usually.

But if Bernie's pushy, Bentley's the opposite. He never has to be pushy, because *he's always right*.

My sister Danika told me I should just hand my money over to him and ask him to invest it. She's not wrong. That would be my best play, hands down, but I want to do something with it myself. No one wants to be a sidekick, right? I mean, not in their own life.

"Remind me again why we're looking at this one." I scrunch up my nose against the blinding rays of the early morning sun, most of my enthusiasm gone now that we're on our fourth day of looking. The old house is elegant, and the lot it sits on is enormous, especially for this area. But it needs a new roof ASAP, as well as a new coat of paint, and that's probably just the beginning. "Our first order of business would be to tear out the enormous and overgrown garden, and that alone feels like a lot of work." If it were well-maintained, maybe, but we've seen places that were bigger and they were in better locations to boot.

We've definitely seen plenty of places that had more rooms. "How many rooms did you say you thought we could get out of it?"

Mostly we've looked at functioning inns. This one's a house we'd have to convert into an inn. More work. More repairs.

More hassle.

No thanks.

"Dave." Bernie sighs. "This is the one I was telling you about last night. It just came back on the market."

I blink, reevaluating. "Wait, you mean the one Audrey Colburn's daughter owns?"

"The one Audrey Colburn lived in her entire married life. The one her *granddaughter* now owns."

"You think that would still be a draw? I mean, I've heard the name, sure, but she was a star back when movies were black and white, right?"

Bernie sighs. "You're so uncultured, and no. Her movies were in color."

"Either way, the number of people who know who she is must be dwindling, right?"

Bernie looks like it's a real imposition to have me as a friend. "It's not about how many people remember her—look. Didn't you say you wanted to change your image?"

I run my hand across my face. "It's not like it's my top priority, though. I mean, I'm sick of being called the garbage guy, but—"

"Nothing says classy like Audrey Colburn. Okay?"

"Fine, but we still evaluate this one with the same criterion as all the others. Total doors matters. We look at likely profit relative to the total cost."

Bernie unlocks the door, and I prepare myself to be impartial. Nothing I see inside will sway me one way or another. I'll tally up the costs and the possible profits, just like I always do, and I'll assign some kind of value to the reputation that comes along with the house and that will be it. I mean, I don't want my future kids to be mocked for having the last name of Fansee and a dad who owns a trash company, but it's not as if that's *all* that matters.

I have to be able to earn a living, too.

The front door creaks as it opens, which doesn't seem promising, but as we walk into a very large, very spacious entryway, I can't help feeling that it's a happy space. That might sound crazy. I mean, it doesn't have the twenty-foot ceilings of the place from last night or the enormous chandelier of that first one by the train station, but it's open, it's bright, and it's clearly got personality. The sunlight streams indirectly from the big bay windows, which all look out onto the wide porch. The wood inside the front rooms is warm and inviting. There are beautiful plaster medallions on the wall and ceiling.

I mean, the trim paint's peeling, the floors are weathered in a few spots, there are dust bunnies making babies, and it smells a little bit like mothballs.

But even so, I like it a lot more than I expected.

We slowly walk the place, now that I'm in a better mood, and we start talking about how many doors we could squeeze out of it, realistically.

"Think of it, though," Bernie says. "The rooms could have names and be themed from her movies. Or the famous people who came and stayed in them, if we could figure that out. This place has history."

"I guess." I study the profit loss sheet. It's still not anywhere near the top of the list there.

"It's an old house," Bernie's still gushing, "but Audrey was ahead of her time. Fourteen of these rooms have bathrooms adjacent to them. Those other four rooms—the study, the library, the sun room, and the music room—could be remodeled to add an en suite bathroom pretty easily. That brings us up to eighteen rooms, and I hear there's a carriage house." Bernie looks as impressed as I feel.

"What's a carriage house?" I feel like I've heard that term before, but I'm not sure what it means.

"It's like a guest house, maybe?" Bernie looks confused. "I think the gardener and chauffeurs used to live there, back before they had power tools and one yard crew could come through and clean this place up in three hours."

The idea of having a live-in gardener at someone's personal residence is mind-boggling to me.

"I wonder why the granddaughter's selling," I say. "You'd think she'd want to stay here, right?"

Bernie frowns. "As I understand it, she has to sell."

"What?" Now I feel a little. . .predatory. "Why?" I need to know more or I'll drown in guilt for someone I don't know.

He shrugs. "Zoning, maybe? It was grandfathered in for years, but now it's transferred to another generation, I heard it can't be a residence anymore."

"Wait, so she's getting kicked out?" Now I feel downright awful. "What happens if she can't sell it?" I follow Bernie out the side door and around a bend, where a cute little one-story house comes into view through a path that's flanked on each side by rows of huge oak trees.

"Would you want to keep a building you couldn't live in and had no other use for?"

I guess not.

"You're doing her a favor," he says. "Stop worrying. Her last sale fell through, and she can't want to keep something she can't even live in. We're not the big bad guy, swooping in and ruining her life. I'm sure she's a pampered little princess, who probably only summered here anyway."

Thinking about it like that, I feel better. I could give this place life. It occurs to me that, although the house was entirely empty in an almost morose way, we could decorate it in the period that Audrey was popular. We could even include placards and prints about her movies on the walls. Then even people who don't care about her at all would get the *feel* of what it means to be in such a graceful and cheerful house.

I've been casting around for the last few days for any kind of theme—really successful inns need themes, apparently—and this is the first one that has felt viable. Once Bernie unlocks the carriage house, I have an epiphany.

"You know, we could make this little house available for family gatherings and private parties. People who want to book a few rooms for privacy, but want the convenience of a shared space. It might make it even more attractive to some people."

Bernie's jotting some notes down, and I'm actually thinking of giving the sprawling green monstrosity a chance, when we hang a right and turn into a large bedroom that must be the master. It's the first room that has been furnished, if you consider a lumpy mattress in the center of the floor furniture. But that's not the biggest surprise.

Not at all.

The biggest surprise is the woman whose head pops up in the center of the mattress, her hair sticking up at strange angles as if she's auditioning for a role in a Dr. Seuss play.

"Buh?" She spins around in the middle of the mattress like she's under attack from all sides. She finally identifies where we are, and blinks repeatedly. "What are you doing here?"

There's a Cheerio stuck to her left cheek, and the other side of her face is covered in pink lines that I assume are from the pressure of the bunched-up sheets being shoved against her face until this very moment.

She drags the errant sheet upward and back over her head with an inelegant groan.

"The listing said the property's vacant," Bernie hisses. "Plus. It's not zoned as residential." He blinks and regroups. "I'm so sorry to invade your space."

"Don't apologize to her," I say. "Obviously she's not

supposed to be here. Call the owner's agent and tell them a vagrant has broken in."

"Vagrant?" When she sits up this time, her voice is so shrill it could practically shatter glass. "*Vagrant?*"

Bernie splutters impressively. "Mr. Fansee didn't mean that."

"Did your footman or whatever just call you Mister Fancy?" She rubs at her eyes. "Or am I dreaming in Disney again?"

"Fan-see," I say, as if pronouncing the word again will explain anything. "Like the word 'fan.' And then the word 'see,' like, what you do with your eyes. But shoved together."

Now the probably-not-homeless woman scowls. "No one told me there was going to be a showing today."

"That's my fault," Bernie says. He's staring at his phone, tapping through things furiously. "I thought I read that it was vacant, and I didn't realize—"

"The listing still clearly indicates that showings must be made in advance and that they're by appointment only." The woman sighs, as if this has happened before. She finally notices the Cheerio, but instead of brushing it away in embarrassment, she plucks it carefully off her cheek. . .and pops it in her mouth. "It's fine." She chews, swallows, yawns, and then stands up.

She's wearing Transformer booty shorts, that I believe were once men's boxers, and a black t-shirt that says, "Stone Temple Pilots" in simple, white, block lettering. There's a large yellow star underneath the name, and someone has written "suck" in black sharpie across the star.

Which means, the message now reads, "Stone Temple Pilots suck."

"It should be 'sucks,'" I say.

"What?" Her brow furrows.

Without the Cheerio to distract me, I can't help noticing how attractive she is. Her long legs, her beautiful, shiny, chocolate hair.

But that's really not why I'm here—ogling a crazy woman. "Stone Temple Pilots is the name of a band, which is a singular entity. So it should be 'sucks.' The descriptor should tie to the plurality of the noun."

When she spears me with a glare, I realize her eyes are so light blue that they're nearly white.

Like tinted ice chips.

That's what they remind me of.

"You woke me up. You called me a vagrant. And now you're correcting the grammar of a t-shirt that's slamming a rock band." She shakes her head and then gestures wildly at the door. "Get out."

"I'm not sure you should say that to someone who's interested in purchasing. . ." Bernie trails off.

"My house?" She drops her hands to her hips. "You may not be sure who I am, but I'm not confused. This property is definitely mine. Now you, get out." She frowns, and then, as if she's very annoyed by having to do it, she tacks on one more word. "Please."

In that moment, I fall hard for this Cheerio-eating, disheveled, feisty, undeniably broken woman. Just like the moment I found that camera twenty years ago, I can't help my overpowering desire to lean forward and pick her up.

I want to fix her. Badly.

Of course, I do manage not to lean toward her or touch her in any way. I'm quite sure she'd punch me, or sue me, or something even worse. But I can't stop staring, and I most certainly don't get out when she orders me. . .please notwithstanding.

"But I want this place," I say.

My real estate agent splutters.

I fold my arms. "This is the one." So much for evaluating it impartially.

"You can't just say that in front of the owner," Bernie hisses. "It destroyed any bargaining power we might have had."

"What do you want for it?" I ask.

"It's listed at five point four million," she says. "So that's what I want. Five point four million."

"But it's not worth that right now," I say. "The roof is about to cave in. The gardens look like a jungle, and the floors have pretty significant signs of wear. Be reasonable."

She huffs. "Do you want it or not?"

"I'm asking how much you'll honestly take for it." I can't help chuckling. "Come on. You're illegally squatting in a place that's not zoned residential, and you're saving last night's dinner on your cheek for a little snack the next morning. You've got to have some wiggle room in that price." Although now that I think about it, she's not really the spoiled princess Bernie said she'd be. Honestly, she looks like she could use the money. Shouldn't Audrey Colburn's granddaughter be fairly well-off?

But what if she's not?

What if she doesn't want to sell, but she *has* to sell? What if she's squatting here because she has nowhere else to go, and no money with which to find a new place until this is gone?

"Well, you were honest with me about wanting it, so I'll come clean, too. I owe the bank a little over two million, thanks to Uncle Sam's taxes and my family's failure to plan for a catastrophic tragedy that left everything to a grandchild—me. Oh, and there's property taxes from last year due, not to mention the fact that we're halfway through this year, and the property taxes are steep. Also, as I assume your agent told you, thanks to some zoning laws, I can't live here anymore unless I'm a live-in manager of some kind of business, which clearly I'm not." Her lower lip wobbles.

I didn't really even have a chance. She's so gloriously damaged that I'm practically itching to fix her. The wobbling lip and the movie-star face are overkill. "How about this? I pay off the bank."

"Huh?" She scratches her head, and somehow it makes her hair stick out in even more directions than before. I wouldn't have thought it possible.

"After that, I'll still have a half million left that we can use to fix it up, buy furniture, and pay the taxes. If you throw in your share in the house, we'll be co-owners, fifty-fifty, and you can help me restore, decorate, and furnish it. Then we can run it as an inn together."

"Is he insane?" the crazy lady asks, clearly addressing Bernie.

"I've thought so for a while," my friend says.

He's so disloyal.

"I'm not insane," I say. "We would own this place free and clear if we went in as equal partners, and you could live here, on property as you are now, only legally, if we listed you as the caretaker. You'd still own your family home, plus you'd get around the zoning laws. The taxes would be easier to pay from here on out, too, with an income. It'd kind of be like having your cake and eating it too, right?"

"Running it as an inn?" She frowns. "It's not big enough. We'd have to call it a bed and breakfast."

"Anything over ten rooms and below twenty-five is usually classed as an inn, and it qualifies. Besides, if we called it a B&B, we'd have to provide a real breakfast," I say.

She shrugs. "Realistically, most inns do that too, don't they?"

"I can't cook," I admit.

"So you hire someone," she says. "But as it happens, I can cook. It's one of the few things I actually do reasonably well."

I'm understandably skeptical of that claim, thanks to the errant Cheerio, but I don't bother arguing. "We can work out the details—like what to call it and what color to repaint it—later. Are you in?"

Bernie's shaking his head desperately, like he's terrified I'm not kidding. "I don't think you can do this—"

I hold up my hand. "It feels a little sudden, but that's how I operate. When I make up my mind, I move ahead, and I have a feeling this is going to help us both."

The woman straightens up, and there's a little spark in her eye, like the power flooding into that camera the very first time I turned it on. It's glorious when something comes back to life, and I'm beginning to think she just needed the reminder of who she is. "I'm Serendipity Audrey Colburn." She pauses then, her eyes lighting up until they're delightfully bright. "But Serendipity's a horrible name for a girl, so I go by Seren."

"Nice to meet you, Seren." I hold out my hand.

She swallows and sighs. "I'm not sure you'll think it was very nice if we go through with this insane plan."

"Why?" I keep my hand extended, and bob it up and down a bit to try and get her to reach out.

"Because you've just met the unluckiest person in the entire world. If you go into business with me, I'll probably just drag you down with me."

"I'm willing to take that risk," I say.

She frowns. "I'll do it on one condition."

"Okay." This would usually be where she'd share what that condition was, so I wait.

"No matter what happens, you vow never to date me." She tilts her head. "If we do this, and we wind up dating, the whole deal's off. I want that put in writing."

I can't keep my lip from twitching. "I may seem hasty, or rash, but surprisingly, I have no trouble finding women to date. I don't need to date my business partner."

"So you agree?" She arches one eyebrow. "If we ever date, the whole partnership will be dissolved in my favor?"

In her favor? What does that mean? "Wait."

"If you want to date me, you'll have to sell your shares to me." She shrugs. "For fair market value."

"If you can get a loan, you mean?" I ask.

"We can let the lawyers work out that part, but it's my family home. If we date, you're the one who walks away."

She's gorgeous. I'll give her that. But I feel like I'll be able to resist the temptation just fine. I like to fix things. I have never once wanted to keep any of the items I repaired. "Sure."

"Well then, Mr. Fancy," she says. "Let's do it." She reaches for my hand.

And when our fingers touch, an electric thrill runs through my entire body that's so shocking, so unexpected, and I almost recant. She drops my hand like a hot potato, so clearly it's not reciprocated.

Which means it'll still be fine. I have a feeling this new chapter in my life, co-owning an inn, is going to be *amazing*. No longer will I be the Garbage Guy.

I'm going into business with Audrey Colburn's granddaughter. It doesn't get much more elegant than that, cheek-Cheerios aside.

SEREN

From the time I was born, people have told me how lucky I am.

"You're so lucky to look just like your grandmother! People would kill for looks like yours."

Except, I have zero interest in being an actress, or a model, or anyone that other people obsess about. I'm the kind of person who was born to hide in my house and pretend I didn't hear the doorbell. That means looks like mine are more of a curse than anything else.

"You're so lucky you don't like chocolate, soda, or candy! It keeps you so thin."

Sure, I'm thin because I don't enjoy the things other people do. Also, whenever it was time for a holiday or a birthday, everyone else would get something. . .and I'd get an apologetic look. "Sorry. I had no idea what to get you." So I got nothing.

"You're so lucky to be naturally athletic."

Except I hate having lots of people look at me, so playing in any kind of sanctioned sporting event was pure torture.

"You're so lucky to be so academically gifted!"

But my amazing grades convinced Mom and Dad that sending me to cooking school would be a mistake. They insisted I attend an ivy league school, which I hated. The only way I learned what *I* wanted to learn was by taking cooking classes at night.

"You're so lucky you were born into a family with so much money."

That one *was* true, at least, until Dad inadvertently mixed pain pills with alcohol and crashed our rental van into a bus on a vacation. The money our family once had disappeared under the weight of so many lawsuits, I couldn't even read through them all.

"You're lucky to be alive."

That's the one I hate more than any other. When your entire family—grandmother, parents, brother, sister, nephews, and husband—all die in an automobile accident, it's not luck to be the sole survivor.

It's a curse.

Every time someone tells me how lucky I am, I want to stab them in the eye with a pitchfork. I want to yank the pitchfork out and throw their excised eyeball on the ground. And then?

I want to stomp on it.

My 'furious and excessive yelling' the third time my boss told me how lucky I was to be alive landed me in an inpatient facility shortly after I returned to work.

That was fun.

After a month of intensive therapy and group sessions, the state of New York, *luckily,* proclaimed me all better.

Goodie.

What I really learned was how to take all my rage

and pain and stuff them deep, deep down so that no one knew they were there.

Hiding in my house helped, too.

What hiding did not help me do was earn enough money to pay the monthly payment on the mortgage that I had to take out thanks to the generational skipping transfer tax. It also did not help me earn money to pay for the utilities or the exorbitant state and local taxes on the mansion. By the time I realized how far behind I was, I was in too deep to do anything about it.

That's when my lawyer—moments before firing me for non-payment—suggested I contact a real estate agent and list the house. It's my one remaining asset of any value, so I ought to sell it before the government or the bank take it from me.

Which is why I'm staring at a crazy guy, who looks an awful lot like a slender Henry Cavill, and who apparently wants to partner with me in turning Grandma's charming, impractical country estate into a bed and breakfast. We'd hopefully be able to pay the taxes, but only because visitors will want to gawk at everything that made her a graceful and admired movie star.

And they'll probably gawk at me too, if they have half a chance.

Basically, my choices are to sell this house and lose the very last thing I have to remind me of my family, or to partner with this loony man who will turn the last thing I have to remind me of my family into something I despise.

Neither option seems too great, if I'm being honest.

Which is how I know it's definitely my life. I'm the queen of not-great options. Instead of naming me

Serendipity, which has turned out to be a real cosmic joke, they should have named me Desdemona, which fittingly means ill-fated. Bonus: it still sounds nice.

Maybe if they'd named me Desdemona, I'd have good luck. Clearly no one has told Mr. Fancy that everything about me spells utter doom. He has no idea he's pitching his idea to the grim reaper of success.

I feel a little bad, but of the two awful options, I think I'd rather ruin something I love than lose it entirely. At least that way, when this plan crashes and burns as it inevitably will, I probably won't be as sad to lose it. Plus, I'll have a legal place to sleep while I wreck this poor man's life with my bad juju.

"We can work out the details—like what to call it and what color to repaint it—later. Are you in?"

His poor real estate agent's shaking his head so hard, I'm worried he'll rattle his brains right out his ears. "I don't think you can do this—"

"It feels a little sudden, but that's how I am," the man says. "When I make up my mind, I move ahead, and I have a feeling this is going to help us both."

He's here looking to buy my family's place, but he really doesn't know my name? "I'm Serendipity Audrey Colburn."

The world's most ironic and absurd name.

That's when it hits me that, for the first time in my life, I don't have to *be* Serendipity. It's a stupid name that never fit me.

I've always hated it.

But like a dog with a new owner that still needs to be able to answer to a name it's heard all its life, I'm scared to jettison it entirely. "But Serendipity's a horrible name for a girl, so I go by Seren."

I let that name roll around in my brain for a bit. Seren.

And then it sinks in, like water disappearing onto dry sand. Just as easily, just as seamlessly, I have a new name. Seren.

I love it.

It's the first thing I've loved in a very, very long time.

"Nice to meet you, Seren." He has unknowingly become the first person to ever call me by my new name. Then he holds out his hand.

He's such a polite, upright-looking guy, and even though he looks like Henry Cavill, he has a different energy somehow.

It hits me then.

He reminds me of Mr. Bingley in *Pride and Prejudice*, with his bubbly, happy, optimistic expressions.

What happens when Mr. Bingley meets Eeyore?

Does the world explode?

I ought to take his hand, but that feels. . .greedy and selfish. Do I really have the right to drag this man down by letting him affiliate with the harbinger of all misery? "I'm not sure you'll think it was very nice if we go through with this insane plan."

"Why?" He's still holding his hand out, and his eyes are encouraging. Did God just send me my own little cheerleader? Or is this just another cosmic joke? I'm sick of waiting for the punch line in my life. It's never funny to be the butt of the joke.

Poor Mr. Bingley deserves some kind of warning, though I might be disappointed if he takes it. "Because you've just met the unluckiest person in the entire world. If you go into business with me, I'll probably just drag you down with me."

"I'm willing to take that risk."

I should tell him no. This deal only really benefits me. Am I really selfish enough to doom him? Then again, my bad luck usually only hurts people who are permanently linked to me.

Like my husband.

I feel like sinking to my knees and bawling. It's been a good half hour since I felt that way, so it's about time. Even so, it's hard to ignore it and stuff that feeling deep, deep down. I can't help letting a bit of it out via a frown.

And then I have an idea. "I'll do it on one condition."

"Okay." He looks. . .curious.

Which is not the goal. I'm trying to warn him and set a boundary that might keep this poor man safe. I try to sound as stern as I possibly can. "No matter what happens, you vow *never* to date me."

Because if he's just a business partner, well. Nothing terrible has ever happened to my bosses or co-workers. But how do I enforce that? A lot of men and women who spend time together wind up falling for each other. What could I say that will keep him safe?

That's when an idea strikes. "If we do this, and we wind up dating, the whole deal's off. I want that put in writing."

"I may seem hasty, or rash, but surprisingly, I have no trouble finding women to date. I don't need to date my business partner." He looks like he thinks it's all some kind of joke, or worse, the start of a cheesy romantic comedy.

I double down again on my sternest look, and I make my tone as fourth-grade-schoolteacher as I can manage. "So you agree?" I arch an eyebrow just like Mrs. Maynard used to do. "If we ever date, the whole partnership will be dissolved in my favor?"

"Wait." Now he's frowning. He's starting to get it, maybe. I mean it, poor Mr. Bingley. Our partnership will *not* turn into some Hallmark movie plot.

"If you want to date me, you'll have to sell your shares." I've made him look nervous. Hold the line, Seren. "For fair market value."

"If you can get a loan, you mean?" he asks.

"We can let the lawyers work out that part, but it's my family home. If we date, you're the one who walks away."

Okay, and now he's decided I'm a complete narcissist, which is fine, I suppose. As long as it keeps him away. "Sure," he says, clearly disillusioned and rethinking his entire proposal.

Actually, it's pretty impressive that I could convince him that I think so highly of myself, given that he initially thought I was homeless. Actually, now that I think about it, I kind of *am* homeless.

"Well then, Mr. Fancy," I say before he changes his mind. "Let's do it." I grab the hand he's still holding out, albeit with much less enthusiasm than before.

When our fingers touch, his eyes widen, and he yanks his hand away. Which is kind of strange. I haven't showered yet, but I don't smell. Much. Why would he recoil like that? That's when I realize that my hands are still sticky from the sugary milk in the bowl of Cheerios I ate before dropping off to sleep last night.

Ugh.

How typical a start for me. Our first partnership handshake, and I'm already ruining it with my gross, late-night snacking habits.

At least he leaves rather quickly after setting up a time for us to meet with his lawyer. I suppose we'll have to see whether he changes his mind, and what kind of language they put in the contract. I've had enough bad experiences with lawyers that I'll believe this is happening when I literally see the terms on the page.

Which reminds me. . .my lawyer fired me. And I'm not dumb, but I'm also no contract guru. I realize I'm going to have to do something I've been avoiding.

Call Corey and ask for help.

It won't be that bad. Honestly. But I hate asking for help, and Corey's always so unintentionally condescending. "Of course you want me to look over this contract," he'll say. "They're confusing, and you should make sure you don't get ripped off."

I mean, that's why I need his help, but I already *know* that's why. The fact that he'll spell it out sort of makes sure I know he's so much better at business than I am.

Maybe I'm just irrationally irritable.

I should be calmer before I call to ask for a favor. I decide to shower and get ready for the day before calling him. That will give me time to prepare for his brand of *I'm the right guy for every job.*

Most girls love it, I know.

He's constantly blanketed with women. I'm lucky to have him for a lifelong best friend. If we hadn't met at that vending machine in elementary school, arguing over who deserved the last package of peanut butter crackers, I have no idea how I'd have survived the Accident.

That's what I call it now.

It gives it an air of mystery and also an elegant feeling of tragedy, I think. Although I doubt anyone else can hear the capital A, in my head, it's clear.

Once I'm showered and my hair is done, I dress for another day of looking for a job. I just need to find one that's okay with hiring a head case. I tap the favorites tab, where I still have a whole row of numbers listed that no longer exist, and I scroll to the bottom.

Corey Fairchild.

I swallow.

Do I really need help? Can't I handle this alone?

I decide to think about it while I look for a job, and I head out the front door. The walk from the carriage house to the garage where my Toyota Camry's parked helps me clear my head, and I feel a little better already. Maybe I won't need help with a contract if it's simple. Maybe it'll just say we're fifty-fifty partners, and that we'll be using Grandma's house as an inn.

Surely I can handle that alone.

When I press the button to open the garage door, the man walking past freezes. It takes me several seconds to realize why.

It's Corey.

"I thought you were in Sri Lanka," I say.

"I came back a week ago," he says. "I've called four times."

I drop my keys on the seat of the car and turn, leaving the door hanging open.

Corey's reached me by now, and he wraps me up in

a tight hug. So many things have changed since third grade, but not this. He feels *safe*. Nothing ever hurts Corey, and nothing changes him, either.

His light brown hair's parted on the right side and combed neatly, the same as always. He's wearing the same pants and sport coat combination he always wears, with his tie a little loosened at the top. His light brown eyes are alert and attentive, just as they always are.

But more than anything else, the thing that defines Corey is his sardonic humor and quintessential lip twist.

"Where are you going?" he asks. "Feel like having a tagalong?" And there it is—his self-deprecatory reference to himself as someone I might not want around.

Although, in this instance, he's right. "I doubt you'd help me at my job interview."

"Why are you interviewing?" His brow furrows. "I thought you loved your job."

I did. It's true. It was very nearly my dream job, except for my boss. "I did," I say. "Until I didn't." I shrug. "Time for something new."

"How long have you been looking?"

I'm way too embarrassed to tell him that, after a generous four-month leave, one week back at work, and a month at the nuthouse, I've been unemployed for the last six months. The last thing I want from Corey is pity. He's probably one of the only people on earth who almost understands how I'm feeling, but unlike me, when his cousin died, he didn't fall apart.

He doubled down on work and became even *more* successful.

"Are you liking your promotion?" I ask. "Or is all the travel too much?"

"I liked it at first. It helped take my mind off Will. But then it started to wear on me." He shrugs. "Doesn't matter now. I got another promotion, and I'll mostly be around. You're looking at the Chief Financial Officer of Harcourt Holdings."

I can hardly believe it. "Whoa, are you serious?" My husband—his cousin—would have been so proud. "That's what you said you wanted. You did it!" I do the math in my head. "And in way less than fifteen years."

"Seven." Corey's sideways smile's back.

"That's amazing, really." I force a smile that I *almost* feel. "But I better head out. My job's not going to find itself."

Corey frowns. "I thought you had an interview."

"More like I plan to have an interview." I tap the side of my head. "Therapist says to envision my success." What a load of crap.

That does not reassure Corey, either. "There can't be that many excellent pastry chef positions in Scarsdale. What're you doing to look?"

This is the part of Corey I hate. If I can't escape, I'll be stuck telling him that mostly I just go to places and try their desserts. I study the menu, and I decide whether they might like my desserts better. . .or whether I might even want to work there. I've only applied at six places in the last six months, and none of them wanted me.

That's also not something I want to tell him.

It's not something I really want to tell anyone.

But Corey knows that while I liked my job, the real reason I loved cooking was because I wanted to cook for my family. I loved making food for big get-togethers. I loved making treats for friends. I loved doing something that no longer needs to be done—because I have no family left.

"We should get together for a meal soon," I force myself to say, when really all I want to do is go back to my gross mattress, eat a bowl of Cheerios, and cry. "I can even cook if you want."

He tosses his thumb over his shoulder. "What's with the FOR SALE sign over there? You're not really selling Grandma's place, right?"

Maybe some things do change. Corey used to feel safe, but right now, talking to him feels like I'm tiptoeing around landmines. I force a nonchalant shrug. "I mean, it's way more space than I need, and—"

"But one day, you may want that space." He looks so doggedly earnest.

"I mean, maybe," I say. "But the taxes are outrageous, and—"

"Just don't rush into anything. I pulled up the listing, and how did you get all those photos of the rooms? They're completely empty! Did you put everything in storage?"

Traveling's a drag, but his absence made some things much easier. He'd have flipped out at the estate sale where people bid on all Grandma's stuff. He'd have absolutely lost it when I settled all those lawsuits against Dad's estate *en masse*, and when I signed over all the proceeds from Grandma's estate to Dad's, as the executor, so the funds could settle them.

If Grandma hadn't died four full days before Dad, it might have been easier, but as it is. . .Everything passed to him, and then on to me. The one asset that was in a trust and went straight to me got hit with the GST. It was all such a huge mess.

Corey would be threatening to sue the lawyers who set it all up, if he knew. But it's not like they were drawing up estate documents with the idea that Dad might cause an epic wave of lawsuits. No one could have predicted what happened in the Accident.

If we could have, it never would have happened. Obviously.

Eventually, he's going to find out about my partnership idea. I may as well brace myself and deal with it now.

Although. To avoid another train wreck in the future, maybe I should enlist his help. Ugh.

"Some people have to rush," I say. "If I don't rush, the bank may take it."

He frowns. "Why would the bank take it?"

I swallow. "There were some lawsuits after Dad. . . And then there was that generation skipping transfer tax on the house. I had to take out a loan."

He blinks. "That's. . .are you sure that's right?"

"Corey, trust me." I can't deal with him telling me I'm an idiot right now. "But I already got an offer, and I'm meeting with the possible buyer tomorrow."

All my plans of looking for a new job evaporate as Corey digs down like a bulldog with his jaws around a sheep's neck. Two hours later, he's still ranting about it. "—could even consider going into partnership with someone you don't even know."

"Then come with me," I say, "to our meeting. Meet him and look over the business plan yourself."

He sits then, his eyes intent on mine. "Why didn't you tell me before?" I hate how hurt he looks. "I could have helped you. I still can. Let me pay off the taxes and get the mortgage up to date, at least. Then you can find a job and make a decision with room to think."

"And I'd owe you *and* the bank, and even when I find a job, I'll never be able to pay all that back. Especially with utilities and repairs on a house like *this*." I sigh. "Corey, do you know what the monthly bills on this place are? Last month, even *vacant*, I owed almost five hundred dollars on the main house just in electricity. And this little cottage house where I'm living cost another hundred and fifty."

"Sure, I get what you're saying, but I can—"

I put my hand on his arm. "You don't get it, because your life is nothing like mine. This is happening. If you want to help me, come to the meeting on Wednesday."

He looks almost sad when he says, "I'll be there."

❄ 4 ❄

DAVE

One time, when I was eleven, I happened to run into my teacher from school at the grocery store.

I was reaching for the perfect apple, which was obviously at the bottom of the pile, when a woman my mother's age took issue and began chewing me out. Almost a full minute into her lecture, I realized who she was.

She had barely looked at my face, so I doubt she recognized me either.

"Mrs. Gant?" I interrupted.

Her eyes widened.

"I can't believe that's you."

Mrs. Gant, you see, always had the most beautiful hair. It was long, it was shiny, and it fell down her back in a waterfall. She also wore perfectly pressed, immaculately tailored clothes, which were so amazing that even kids at the school talked about them. She wouldn't let us use pens in class, because once a kid accidentally made a dark mark on one of her fancy cream blouses. Mrs. Gant wore stylish shoes too, tall boots and trendy high heels, cute sneakers and strappy sandals.

She *did not* have dark circles under her eyes and frizzy hair, glasses that slid down her nose, and baggy grey sweatpants. In a million years, I'd never have even fathomed that she would wear a huge old t-shirt, bunched up at the waist and half-tucked into the sweatpants.

But of course, that's what she was wearing and that's how she looked that day at the store. As an adult, I can understand how that happens. My mother would take great care to apply her makeup each morning, and she usually took the time to curl her hair with hot rollers. But occasionally, with nothing to do and nowhere to go, she'd skip all that work and just be. With the perspective of an adult, the shocking difference between the teacher who taught me reading and writing and science and the woman who shouted outrageously over the right way to remove an apple from a stack wasn't as shocking.

But that day? I was poleaxed.

I later discovered that Mrs. Gant had a crush on the PE coach and all that impressive effort was to make sure she caught his eye. It worked. They were married right before I graduated from elementary school, and everyone at the school kept talking about it.

In all the years between then and now, I've still never seen a transformation quite as marked as the one Mrs. Gant—now Mrs. Meade—made from her personal shopping persona to her business one.

Until today.

When Seren Colburn walks through the door to

meet with me and review the agreement I had drawn up, I don't even recognize her at first.

What I previously thought might be a passing resemblance to her famous grandmother, I now see is an uncanny likeness. Her dark hair's pulled back into a smooth and elegant French twist. Her thick eyebrows arch perfectly over dark, fringed lashes, which frame up huge, expressive eyes. Her nose has a perfect aristocratic arch.

But her lips?

The bright red lipstick she applied really makes the full shape of them stand out, and contrasted with her angular face and highlighted with her sleek, little black dress and conservative black pumps?

She looks like she walked off the set of a movie. Literally. She's even holding an ebony clutch with a large gold clasp. It's utterly impractical, which only adds to the air of elegance and grace.

"We could just use your image as our billboard ad," I say. "Talk about selling the memory of your grandmother."

She blinks, looking even more adorable when she's confused. "Are we planning on selling the memory of my *dead* grandmother?"

I sputter. "I mean, that's kind of the draw to using the house as—"

She laughs then, and the sound is like children playing in the street—open, joyful, and refreshing. "I'm kidding. Of course I know that."

"But you should really be more sensitive." For the first time, I realize she didn't come alone. Just behind and to the left of Seren, there's an utterly forgettable man in a navy suit. He's buttoned and combed and slicked and looks like the quintessential businessman, and I hate him on sight.

"Sensitive?"

The man frowns. "Serendipity has been through—"

"Seren," I say. "She goes by Seren." I frown. "You did come in with her, did you not?"

Bafflingly, that makes Seren blush. "It's fine," she says. "Corey's an old friend."

"You're going by Seren now?" His tone is low —intimate.

It makes me want to spill my coffee all down his stupidly expensive tie. He looks exactly like the kind of person who called me Garbage Guy all those years.

"I felt like I needed. . .something new." She swallows, and I can't look away from her. She looks utterly vulnerable for some reason, and I can't figure out why.

The Suit smiles. "I think it's a wonderful idea."

"You do?"

And now I'm being left out at my own meeting. "Right over here," I say. "I wish I'd known your lawyer was coming. I'd have had them print out an extra copy."

"That's alright," the Suit says. "We're fine sharing." He shifts his seat closer to her, and I want to kick it back out.

But Seren doesn't seem to mind.

"Bernie!" I hate how shrill my voice sounds. I clear my throat and make sure it comes out deep and manly this time. "We need another copy in here."

The Suit *laughs*, as if he knows just why I've screamed for one.

"I'm not her lawyer," he says, slinging his arm over the back of her chair and leaning pointedly closer. "I'm her oldest friend. She asked me to come for moral

36

support, but also because I'm the Chief Financial Officer of an investment capital firm and pretty familiar with contracts and sneaky business strategies."

"Nothing sneaky here," I say.

"I guess we'll see." The Suit looks smug.

"It's surprising you have time to come here," I say, "on a random Wednesday. You'd think the CFO of a big investment firm would be too busy." I pick up the contract. "But I guess not."

He laughs again, and I realize that I don't hate him.

I *despise* him.

More than I disliked Barney when I was a kid, more than I hate the New York Knicks, more, even, than I abhorred the man who broke my sister's heart back in high school, I loathe the Suit.

"And what's your job history?" the Suit asks. "What qualifies you to go into partnership with my *Seren*?"

I'm definitely going to spill coffee on him. *My* Seren? He didn't even know she was going by that name two minutes ago, but now he owns her? He probably was busy, but he canceled it all. He moved his important meetings and he held all his calls, just so he could run over here and drape himself over her. He's like a dog, peeing on his favorite fire hydrant so that all the other dogs—I'm realizing this makes me a dog, too—won't mistake it for an unclaimed one.

But obviously she isn't his. There's no ring on her finger.

The Suit's still looking at me expectantly and I remember he asked me a question. How am I qualified to be her partner.

"I assume you mean, other than the fact that I have the business capital she needs to pay off her mortgage and repair and remodel the house?" I can't help glaring a little.

"Other than money, what qualifies you?" the Suit asks. "Because you're not the only person in New York with money. You're not even the only person in the room."

I wonder how far this pencil would go into his eye before it hit his brain. . . "I ran my dad's company for the past decade, and now that he's transitioned to a more rural area, I've decided to branch out on my own. But if you're asking about my education, I went to NYU for college, and I studied business."

"Isn't that where Jacob went?" Seren asks, clearly missing all the subtext. "Or did he go to Columbia? It was in the city, I'm sure."

"I haven't talked to Jacob since my freshman year at Harvard," the Suit says, name dropping that his school beat my school.

"That's too bad," she says. "I've lost touch with him too." She sighs, and then she glances down at the thick contract. Her eyes are bright, and she looks. . .optimistic. Much more so than when we met. "This is a lot longer than I expected." She bites her full bottom lip, and my heart lifts. She looks. . .intent. "Shall we start?"

Could she be excited about this? As excited as I am?

Fixing up the old mansion and converting it to an inn has so much potential, and now I'm realizing that my partner has even more potential than I initially recognized.

"We should," I say.

Thankfully Bernie finally shows up with the extra

document, and he and my overpriced lawyer sit down right on cue.

Her stupid Suit, whose name I refuse to ask for, actually provides a lot of helpful insight as we walk through the agreement, waving off her concerns on standard contract provisions and explaining how they work and why they're phrased as they are. I still hate him, but it does seem that he's fairly business savvy. He doesn't even seem bent on torpedoing the deal.

Until we reach the dating clause.

Which I kind of understand. My lawyer thought I was kidding when I told him to include it.

"Section seventeen will require my client to—" My lawyer clears his throat and shakes his head. "Sell his shares for fair market value to Miss Serendipity Audrey Colburn—"

"Wait," the Suit says. "Colburn? Not Fairchild?"

Seren winces.

"When did you change your name?" he asks.

She swallows, looking down at her hands.

"The paperwork you submitted to our office," my lawyer says, "indicated that your last name was Colburn. Is that not correct?"

"It is." Her voice is so small, I could tuck it in my handkerchief pocket.

"But to change your name—"

"You seem to be upsetting Seren," I say. "Maybe you should step outside for a moment."

The Suit stands up. "Why? So you can keep twisting her arm until she signs on for this ridiculous arrangement? She shouldn't even be selling that house, not after what she's been through. If you had a shred of decency—"

"Corey." She shakes her head, but it's such a small motion that it's barely visible.

He stops like he was hit with a freeze ray.

"Don't."

"Don't what? Who is this guy? He doesn't even know your last name's Fairchild."

"It's not." Seren finally looks up, her eyes sparking. "I never changed it, okay? I kept meaning to, but then we had that trip out of the country, and I didn't have time to change my name and get a new passport in time. Then after. . ."

"After what?" I ask.

"The Accident," the Suit and Seren say at the same time.

"The accident?" I ask.

"When her grandmother and her parents died," Bernie hisses. "Remember? I told you—"

"I'm so sorry for your loss," I say. "But what does that have to do with your name?" It's been more than a year. I mean, people struggle when they lose parents. I can't even imagine losing mine, but why would her name change?

"It wasn't just her parents who died in the Accident," the Suit says. "It was also her husband." His lips are compressed into a thin line.

Because I'm an insensitive jerk. I should have looked into news reports. I feel horrible, now. She hadn't changed her name to *his*, which means they were probably newlyweds.

Ugh.

My lawyer recovers before I do. "I hate to be asking this, but I just want to confirm that Colburn is the correct name for this paperwork. Right?"

There's a special place in hell for lawyers. There must be.

"Really?" the Suit asks. "That's your next question? You draft a weird agreement with stipulations about her being forced to buy all his shares if they *date*, and then you find out her husband died a little over a year ago, and now you just plow ahead with confirming her name?"

"Corey," she whispers. "I asked for that clause about the shares. You're the one who's making it awkward."

Burned. He drops into his chair like a squirrel whose branch snapped. His eyes are still open and alert, but he definitely didn't see that coming. "Oh. Why?"

"I'm entering into this under the provision that Mr. Fancy and I can never date."

"Fancy?" Corey looks lost.

"You seem to have trouble with last names," I say, suddenly irritable without being sure quite why. Maybe because I feel like an idiot. Maybe because I don't like the idea of her telling *him* that she and I can't date. Or maybe I'm just annoyed at being stuck in close proximity to this guy. He makes me feel all itchy, like I feel when I'm stuck in the same house as a cat. I'm mildly allergic, so it makes my nose itch and my eyes water.

Only, around the Suit, it makes my hands itch to make *his* eyes water. And his nose bleed.

"Let's just keep going," Corey says. "I'm sorry for making it into such a big deal."

"Yes," Seren says. "Let's move past it."

I expected this process to take days—weeks, even —but instead, we resolve it that afternoon.

"I can make these changes right now," my lawyer

says. "I could have documents ready for you to sign in twenty minutes."

"But what about the bank?" Seren asks. "Don't we need to—"

"We're not purchasing a property that requires us to take out a loan," I say. "We're forming a partnership, and I have the contribution capital right now. Since I'm adding cash, and you're adding real property subject to a lien, we both sign documents to create the partnership, and then we complete the other forms as they come."

"After you sign, though," Corey says, "you're obligated to contribute the house, so it's like you're selling it."

"Sure," I say. "That's true."

"Are you sure you want to do this?" he whispers. "Because I'm more than happy to—"

She shakes her head. "I'm sure."

He exhales and looks away.

"Where do I sign?"

And just like that, it's done. Seren and I are in business together. All too soon, she's marching out the door, and then she's gone.

"I can't believe you just did that," Bernie says.

"Why not?" I ask. "The more I found out, the better I felt about it. She's not a raving lunatic who's stealing tiny Cheerios boxes from local hotels to eat while trespassing. She cleaned up pretty well."

"Too well." Bernie frowns. "But that's not what I mean."

"Huh?"

"After we spent more than a week looking at places, I can't believe you went and just created a partnership, robbing me of my three percent." Bernie's acting like it's a joke, but I realize he's actually annoyed.

If he weren't so rich that he owned three sports cars and a Hummer—in New York City—I might feel a little worse. As it is, I don't really feel bad for my greedy friend having wasted his time. I clap a hand on his shoulder. "How about this?" I ask. "When we open, you can come stay for free, any weekend you want." I lean closer. "You can even bring a friend."

He rolls his eyes and heads for the door, but in the process, he kicks something. He bends over and stands up, holding a small black tube. "What's this?"

I extend my hand and examine the lipstick. *Ruby Red*. It must be hers. "Looks like it fell out of Miss Colburn's purse. I have to drive to Mom and Dad's later. I'll just drop it off."

Bernie frowns. "You're just looking for an excuse."

"For what?"

"To see her again. I noticed today."

"Noticed what?"

"You're the biggest idiot I know, drawing up a document that'll let her buy you out after you've put in all the work."

"She can't buy me out," I say. "Unless—"

Bernie's shaking his head as he walks out. "Yeah, unless you're stupid enough to date her, which clearly, you totally are."

"She has to buy me out," I shout. "It's not as if she just gets the whole thing!"

The secretary who walks by shoots me a very strange look.

Even that doesn't stop me from heading straight for Colburn Mansion, like a junkie beelining to his dealer. Could Bernie be right? Do I want to date her? Am I a total idiot?

No.

I do not want to date her.

She's a pampered princess who's now faced with reality after her family died. She's also, apparently, a widow who will be grieving for the next *who knows* how long.

I don't want any of that. I like to fix things, but I don't fall for the things I fix. Usually, once I've repaired something, I give it to someone else to use. I feel much better as I park my car on the curb and text her that I'm here with the lipstick she forgot.

LEAVE IT IN THE MAILBOX.

It's springtime. Sometimes it gets up to the eighties by midday. Is she kidding? It'll melt.

IT'S HOT. I'LL JUST BRING IT IN, I text back.

A few seconds later, the gate to the property opens, allowing me entry. As I trot through the massive iron gate, I think about how differently we must've been raised. She was immensely wealthy, which has clearly changed, and she grew up in a family that had private gates and acres of gardens, right in the middle of Scarsdale.

Meanwhile, I grew up with a dad who worked his way up from hauling trash to managing a crew to starting his own landfill. While he's done quite well, I remember when money was tight. And my dad didn't even graduate from high school. My parents pushed me to go to a good school, and I'm proud of my degree from NYU.

But dating this woman would be idiotic for even more reasons than the risk to my business venture. She belongs with someone like the Suit, who no matter how clueless she is, clearly really likes her. Someone who went to Yale or Dartmouth and who wears suits all the time.

Not someone who spent his summers dumping garbage cans to save for college before lucking into a half-tuition scholarship.

"Dave?"

I'm standing on the beautiful front porch of the Colburn estate. It doesn't seem real that I'm about to own half of it.

I spin around.

Seren's standing just past the edge of the porch, through the landscaping, one eyebrow raised as she stares at me with her head cocked. "What are you doing?"

I shake my head. "I guess I forgot you live in the gardener's house or whatever."

She laughs. "We always called it the Cottage, and I grew up there, actually. Dad hated it, but Mom loved being on such a fancy estate. She was upset when he finally insisted we buy our own place. I was fourteen."

"Oh."

She circles and walks up the steps to the front porch, and then she extends her hand.

I stare at her. What does she want?

"My lipstick?" She looks concerned, now.

"Right. Duh." I pull it out of the pocket of my slacks and hand it over.

"Thanks. It's hard to find this color, so I'm glad you noticed it." I realize that she's changed clothes, and she looks somewhere in between "Stone Temple Pilots Suck" and "dynastic elegance."

This might be my favorite version of Seren yet.

Her hair's down, but it's been brushed. It's shifting

gently in the wind. Her eyes are wide and clear, like a summer sky. She's wearing jeans and a white lace top that looks. . .effortless.

And expensive.

"Did you need something else?" she asks. "We were going to circle back when the paperwork has all gone through, but we could walk the house now and talk about the changes we want to make if you'd rather."

"Actually, I called a list of contractors and they're supposed to come out on Saturday. Will that work?"

She shrugs. "Sure, if you think that'll give us enough time to know what we want before we ask them to do it."

Before I can explain my reasoning, my phone rings. I hold up one finger and check the screen. Leslie. I suppress my groan. I don't want to answer, but she'll just keep calling and calling.

"Girlfriend?" she asks.

"One second." I turn around as I take the call, as if that will somehow keep Seren from hearing anything. "Hey. I'm working. What do you want?"

"What do I want?" Leslie asks. "You'd think I was an insurance salesman instead of your girlfriend."

"You're not my girlfriend," I whisper. "We went out twice. A month ago."

"You took me to see the Mets."

I grit my teeth. "The *Yankees*."

"Whatever."

I hate the Mets almost as much as I hate Leslie. "I've already asked you to stop calling, more than a dozen times. I blocked your number, and you bought a new phone."

"Correction. I *lost* my phone," she says. "I *had* to get a new one."

"You changed your number so you could call me again," I say. "Look, I'm about to block you. Again. If that doesn't work, we're looking at a restraining order."

"Why are you whispering?" Her voice escalates. "Are you with another woman?"

I hang up, and I block her again. I wonder how long it will be before she calls me from another number this time.

"That sounded intense," Seren says.

"You know, no one takes stalking seriously when a woman's the one doing it," I say. "I feel like it should be just as serious, even if she can't physically overpower me."

"So do I," she says. "Call the cops."

I sigh. "Eventually, she's got to let go, right?"

"Or she'll kill your future wife," Seren says. "Which I assume is not going to be her."

I can't help chuckling. "Not unless I go insane."

"Dating's horrible," Seren says. "I'm glad I never have to do it again."

"Oh?"

She shrugs. "I got married once. Been there. Done that."

"You're never going to date again?" Is that why she included it in the contract? Because now it feels like some of the damage, and I'm itching to fix it.

But I cannot date her.

I know this.

"You should get out there," I say. "Even if the first few dates are just awful."

"You sound like my friend Barbara. She kept saying the same thing, so I went on three dates last month. It had been over a year, and she insisted it was time."

"Sounds like a smart lady."

"I used to think so."

I chuckle. "They didn't go well, I take it?"

"Well, no one's stalking me." She's smiling.

"What happened?" I lean against the porch column.

"First one asked about my dead husband. I started out fine, just saying how great he was, but then I started bawling and couldn't stop."

"So that's a dead end." It's a bad joke. I regret it the second I make it.

Seren stares at me for a moment, wide-eyed, and then she starts laughing, the largest laugh I've ever heard from a woman. She keeps laughing until tears are rolling down her cheeks.

When she finally stops, she's shaking her head. "No one ever makes jokes about it."

It feels like I narrowly missed my execution. "I'm glad I could buck the trend."

"Everyone's always so serious and so sad when they find out. They act like I'm made of porcelain and will break at the slightest bump. I'm already serious and sad naturally, so I don't need anyone making it worse. But yeah, that setup was DOA."

"And the other two?"

"Eh, one guy was as interesting as a box of Kleenex, and the other guy was so OCD I knew I'd drive him up the wall before the date ended. The second time he adjusted my napkin, I told him I had an emergency and left."

"Who set you up with these losers?" I ask.

She smiles. "My friend Barbara introduced me to the guy who had to put up with me bawling, and my friend Corey found the other two."

"There's your problem," I say. "That Suit likes you. Of course he introduced you to duds."

"Corey?" She rolls her eyes. "I've known him since we were small children. He's my husband's cousin. He's the reason Will and I met, actually."

I'll just bet he is. And I would also bet that Corey hated that cousin the second the poor guy hit it off with Seren. "Look, if you met some decent guys, you might not hate dating so much. I'd even be willing to take you out on a double date, and I have an idea of a guy you might like."

"You have an idea?" She arches one eyebrow. "That sounds dangerous."

"Unless me setting you up counts as 'dating.'" I cross my index fingers and hold them in front of my face. "I don't want to run afoul of any contract provisions."

"And what kind of girl should I find for you?" she asks.

"Anyone who won't stalk me if we don't hit it off is fine," I say. "And maybe someone who likes the Yankees."

"Who else would she like?" Seren asks.

"The Mets?" I cringe just saying it.

"What about someone who doesn't care about sports?" She tilts her head.

"That might be worse."

She laughs. "Then my confession will probably help us follow the rules, because you've never met someone who cared less about sports in your life. But I have a friend who's a huge Yankees fan, and she loves outdoorsy stuff, too. You seem like an outdoorsy guy."

I nod. "Guilty."

"Alright," she says. "It's not a violation if you're setting me up and I'm setting you up, right?"

"Even though we're going out together?"

"As long as you promise to keep me from spending the entire date crying, then I'll allow it."

I hold up my arm, palm out. "Scout's honor."

"There's no way you're a boy scout."

"I certainly was. At least, I was for long enough to learn that there's a thing called Scout's honor," I say. "But not much more than that."

"I knew it."

"How?"

"You're not nerdy enough," she says.

For some reason, that makes me just a little bit proud. Not that I care what she thinks.

"How about Friday night?" I ask. "We can both check and see if our setup candidates are free."

She shrugs. "Sure."

"Can I snap a photo?"

She frowns. "Why?"

"Let's just say that my friend Bentley is usually busy, but if the girl's pretty enough, he finds time."

"Does that mean I'm pretty enough?" She makes the worst duck face I've ever seen.

"If you never do that again, you are."

She laughs, and that's when I snap the photo.

Bentley texts me back less than ten seconds later.

"He's in," I say.

"Barbara says she's free, too."

"You're setting me up with your dearest friend?"

"Only," she says, entirely serious, "if you promise to be nice. Because she's my only friend, other than Corey."

I want to wrap her in bubble wrap and carry her

50

around in my pocket to make sure no one ever hurts her again. "Is she cute?"

She shrugs. "She's tall, thin, and she has big boobs."

"You could've just said yes."

She laughs, and I decide that Bernie may be right, but not for the reasons he thinks. I may be addicted to her laughter, but that doesn't mean I want to date her. I just want to see her restored to her proper glory.

There's a difference.

❧ 5 ❧

SEREN

A long time ago, movies were made exclusively in black and white. By the time my grandmother became famous, they were all in color, of course, but I know a lot about early movies, thanks to her. Plenty of her mentors and friends remembered the days before color.

My life was in color for twenty-five years.

After the accident, it just went monochrome. Every day blurred together. Food all tasted the same. The sun came up and went back down, but it didn't really impact me.

Barbara worried that I'd lost weight, but I knew it didn't really matter. Food was just fuel—which wasn't something I believed until the Accident. I loved food before. It was the center of my life, right next to my family. I loved it because of the color and texture it brought, and the feelings it enhanced.

I waited and waited and waited for color to come back. I wanted to care about my life, about what happened, about what didn't, but I just couldn't bring myself to do it. When I did care, it landed me in even more trouble, like when I raged out on my boss and wound up in the psych ward.

Until Mr. Fancy showed up.

Something snapped into view that morning. His accusations that I was a trespasser, his proposition that we go into partnership, and now his challenge that I go on a date with someone decent. . .they all woke me up in a way I haven't been awake in over a year. I can't decide whether it excites or frightens me.

But both of those are a feeling, at least.

And those feelings have me thinking about the past. About the things I used to do, the job I used to love, and the people I used to see all the time. My parents were bright and bubbly and vivacious. My mother loved flowers—arranging them, tending them, all of it. She worked at a florist's shop, not because she had to, but because she loved it. My dad worked at his father's company, and he was pretty good at it, I think. My brother was all queued up to take over for him. My sister was a lawyer, and she had just hung out her shingle when she had twin boys. She meant to re-enter the work force a few weeks after the Accident. Her sons were all power trucks and dinosaurs and bugs and barking dogs and anything and everything scary and manly and tough.

I don't usually think about them, because it usually takes me to the dark place. It usually means I don't want to talk or walk or move. I usually wind up crying for hours or days after thinking about what I had. What I've lost.

As I get ready for this date, I think about all of them. Even Will. My husband was not tall, dark, or especially handsome.

In fact, my parents didn't understand why I fell for him at all.

My grandmother hated him for a long time.

But he was brilliant, the nation's foremost expert on the impact of wind shear on sky scrapers. He was also generous. He was hard-working. And most of all, he was unfailingly kind. Not the 'nice' that people say about everyone when they have nothing else to say.

You really find out what kind of person someone is when they're tired. When they're frustrated. When their dreams have been squashed. And no matter the situation, no matter the person, Will was always, always kind. Even when he was tired, disappointed, or angry, he was still polite and considerate of others.

There aren't many people like that in the world.

Other than my family, everyone who met him loved him. His boss, the Department Chief of Engineering at Columbia, the other professors, and his students all saw him for what he was: someone who made the lives of everyone else around them better.

I've always thought that if I ever did remarry, it would be to someone like him.

The man Dave set me up with appears, at first glance, to be Will's polar opposite. His somewhat longish hair still looks perfectly coiffed. His teeth are large, white, and perfectly straight. His smile tells me he knows he's attractive. He has an athletic build that screams of hours spent with a personal trainer. And his clothing looks professionally coordinated to fit the term 'business casual.'

"You made it," he says as Barbara and I exit her Tesla and walk toward the hostess station. "It's a pleasure to meet you." He holds out his hand, like we're meeting to discuss a merger.

I want to ask how he knows it's me without Dave there to tell him, but then I recall Dave snapped a photo.

"Um, yes. I'm Seren." I don't shake his hand. I'm not interviewing for a job.

"I'm Barbara." She's smiling big enough for both of us, and she offers her hand.

Ironically, when he shakes it, he looks a little annoyed.

"I hear you like to cook," he says, making it clear he's here to meet me, not her.

It might be flattering if I already liked him, but for some reason it feels rude.

Dave jogs up before I can say anything. He clearly did not valet.

"Really?" Bentley asks. "You still won't valet?"

"I worked hard to earn the money for that car. I'm not going to pass it off to some high school dropout."

"It's a Honda Accord," Bentley says. "It might look *better* with a few dings."

That does make me laugh. Not because I think there's anything wrong with Hondas, but it is a funny car to stress about valeting.

"I'm Barbara," my best friend says. "I run a yoga studio."

"You know, you *look* like someone who would run a yoga studio," Dave says. "I bet you can twist yourself into a pretzel and then hold yourself up with one hand."

Barbara smiles. "Actually, I don't do yoga at all. My crazy mom started the studio, but she's terrible with business, so I manage it for her. I'm a runner, and I'm really, really inflexible."

55

In more ways than one. Barbara's *not* the kind of woman who just agrees with people about anything.

"I'm a runner too," Dave says. "And I'm horrible about never stretching before I get started."

"Looks like we have that in common." Barbara walks alongside him as we enter, tossing me a wink over her shoulder.

Obviously she's pleased with the setup so far.

"Should we find a different table?" Bentley mock whispers. "One for people who don't love misery?"

I follow Barbara and Dave, assuming he's kidding, but it does make me laugh. "You know, Barbara was my roommate in college, and she woke me up every morning for two months straight to ask whether I wanted to go running with her. Finally, once I actually got up and went with her."

"Once?" Bentley raises his eyebrows.

"Yeah," I say. "She never asked me again."

This time, he laughs—a great big belly laugh I did *not* expect from someone who looks that polished.

"I've always thought runners had something wrong with their brain chemistry," he says.

"You don't look out of shape, though," I say.

"Says the woman who weighs a buck."

I snort. "I wish. At least ten or fifteen more than that."

"Yes, because that's a significant difference." We've reached the table, and Bentley pulls out my chair for me. "Besides. Dave's sister Danika told me that all women subtract ten pounds from their real weight when they share it." He drops his voice. "Did you not get the memo?"

Alright. Maybe he's nothing like my husband, but he is pretty funny. "I guess not."

Dave picks up his chair and slams it against the floor so loudly that a waiter rushes over. "Is there something I can get all of you to drink?"

"I think my friend here needs a 'chill out' cocktail. Do you have one of those?" Bentley smirks.

"Two of those," Barbara says.

"I'll have the McAllen Oak 18," Bentley says. "I called ahead to make sure you had it."

"A connoisseur," Barbara says.

"Bentley knows more about McAllen whiskey than anyone you've ever met," Dave says.

"It's because my first reorg project out of business school was for them." Bentley's smile is very satisfied. I can't tell whether it's in anticipation of a good drink, or because he's proud of being a recognized expert.

"And for the lady?" the waiter asks.

"Just water for me," I say, "with lemon, if you have it."

"Water?" Dave asks. "Come on. Bentley's happy to pay. Get whatever you want."

"I want water," I say.

"Actually, water for me too," Bentley says. "I've been meaning to cut back on my alcohol for years, but now it seems like I have a little more inspiration than usual."

"Do you drink usually?" Dave asks. "Because we'll happily call you a cab or an uber."

I shrug. "Nope. Never."

"Really?" Dave looks shocked.

Then again, most people would probably be shocked.

"But she doesn't mind if we do," Barbara says. "Just as long as we do this." She tosses me her keys. I left my car at her house for this very reason. If she wasn't so proud of her car, I'd have just driven. But for a blind date she's excited about, Barbara cares a great deal about making a good first impression. "There are some perks to having Serendipity as a best friend."

"Seren—what?" Bentley asks.

"Ah, sorry," Barbara says. "I mean Seren."

"What did you say, though?" Bentley asks.

"It's my full name," I say, "but I hate it. My parents named me that so I'd have good luck, but it back-fired." I better rein it in, or Bentley's going to check me back into the loony bin. "I only decided last week to go by Seren, so my friends are having trouble changing gears."

"Luckily, you really only have two of us," Barbara says. "I'm sure we'll get it straight soon enough."

And that's the perfect example of what people are always saying to me. "Luckily this" and "luckily that" when what they really mean is something *unlucky*. I only have two friends, so changing my name isn't a very big deal.

Bentley looks a little shell-shocked, and I'm guessing that means Dave didn't tell him about the dead family and husband. I actually prefer when other people have already told someone for me. When I tell them myself, I get a lot of awkward looks, even more awkward attempts at condolences, and there's an inevitable lull in the conversation that falls to *me* to fix. Somehow having a tragedy in my past never stops haunting me.

"Well, now you have four," Dave says. "Assuming you still like us after a few drinks."

But I notice that when they arrive, the only person who drinks any alcohol is Barbara. Dave's sits untouched.

"You guys can all drink," I say. "Honestly, it's fine. I know you were excited about that McAllen 18, or whatever."

"Is there a reason you don't drink?" Bentley asks.

"Can I take your order?" The waiter looks around the table slowly. "Is everything alright?"

"Oh, I was just telling them how my dad had a drink before driving and managed to kill my entire family and a bus full of people. I was the only survivor, and now I don't drink. But I do love lasagna. Like, I love it so much that it's sometimes all I can think about. I'd like the five cheese one." I hand him my menu.

The waiter tilts his head because he can't decide whether I'm kidding. Perversely, this has become my defense against the awkward silences that seem to follow me everywhere.

I can't quite keep the corner of my mouth from turning up. If Will's watching this from heaven right now, he'd be smiling, too.

"I'll have the lasagna too," Dave says. "I still haven't found any that's as good as my mom's, but I'm always trying."

"Did she die, too?" Barbara asks.

"Not unless the HOA president finally strangled her over some unapproved landscaping," Dave says, "but if I want her lasagna, I have to undergo the interrogation about whether I'm dating and when I'll finally get married."

"And she'll try to set you up again." Bentley offers his menu to the waitress. "I'll have the gnocchi and also the chicken Parmesan."

"Hang on," the waiter says. The poor guy looks a little overwhelmed. "Do you want the five cheese

59

lasagna as well?" He's looking at Dave. "Or the regular kind?"

"Wait, five cheese?" Dave asks. "I bet the regular's way better."

"Seren's also a vegetarian," Barbara says.

"You are?" Bentley asks.

"Oh, no. What died this time?" Dave asks. "Let me guess. Bambi."

Bentley kicks him under the table.

But I burst out laughing. Again.

Dave's the first person who isn't moping around me, who isn't walking on eggshells, but he's still acknowledging that it sucks.

"No, although watching Bambi was scarring."

"What, then?" Bentley asks.

"I know this one," Barbara says. "When Serendip —er, when Seren was a little girl, her parents explained that chicken, the food, is called chicken because it comes from a dead chicken, and that was it. She was done." Barbara shrugs. "From that day forward, she wouldn't eat meat. No chicken. No cows. No pork."

"Wait, as a tiny kid?" Bentley asks. "That's pretty impressive."

"No way my parents would have let that fly," Dave says. "I'm pretty sure they'd have locked me in my room until I was forced to eat Dad's burned grilled chicken or I starved."

"I'm lucky mine were more accommodating," I say.

"Did you want to place your order?" the waiter asks.

"Right," Barbara says. "I'll have the veal."

I can't help my cringe.

"Someone has to offset all the good you put out into the world," Barbara says.

"It's a baby," I say. "Veal's a *baby* cow."

"A *delicious* baby," Barbara says. "And I appreciate its sacrifice."

I notice that, when the food comes, Dave and Barbara tear into theirs, but Bentley's not eating his chicken parmesan. Just his gnocchi. "You can eat it, you know," I say. "I'm not one of those annoying vegetarians that, like, throws paint on people's fur."

He smiles. "I can tell, but that's just it. All the things you say make me think, 'hey, Bentley. That stuff you always say you should do but don't? This gorgeous, smart woman actually does them.' And then I want to do them, too."

"You're kidding, right?" Dave says. "I've never once heard you say you wanted to give up meat."

"I also haven't told you that I want to get married on the beach," Bentley says. "Dudes don't talk about that stuff. Doesn't mean it's not true."

Dave rolls his eyes. "I'll make sure to book some time for next week to talk about all your hopes and dreams. You know, the stuff I've ignored, like your desire to stop drinking and stop consuming animal flesh."

Bentley glares at Dave, and I wonder if this is how they usually behave, or if it's a weird dynamic for them to be on a double date together.

"Is your lasagna good?" Dave asks. "Because mine's not quite *Mom's*, but it's a close second."

"I'm glad," I say. "Mine is fine."

"You could try one little bite of mine," Dave says. "I won't tell anyone."

"Okay," I say. "Sure."

"Wait, really?" Dave's eyes light up. "Cool." He

spears a large bite and holds it out toward me, his free hand underneath it in case it drips.

"Oh, I'm so excited to have my first bite of meat in twenty-six years. No one has ever asked me before, but all this time, I've been dying to change my mind about something I felt strongly about at age two."

"Are you kidding?" Dave's arm drops a bit.

"No dude, keep holding it up. Any minute now she'll eat it." Bentley chuckles.

Barbara slaps the table and laughs, far too loudly. "That's so funny. You guys are hilarious."

That's when I notice her cheeks are also bright pink.

"How much has she had to drink?" I ask.

Dave shrugs. "I wasn't keeping track."

"Too many." I wave at the waiter, point at her drink, and wave my index finger at him.

He nods, thankfully.

Barbara would be horribly embarrassed tomorrow if I let her keep drinking when no one else was. I don't just hold her keys. I also keep her from going overboard.

"Who wants dessert?" Barbara asks.

"Actually, Seren doesn't eat dessert," Dave says. "It encourages people to become addicted to sugar, and that's the root cause of war worldwide."

"You know nothing," Barbara says. "Serendipity *loooooves* dessert."

"I was just guessing," Dave says.

"Well, you were wrong." Barbara leans against his arm and pats it. "Sooooo wrong."

"Oh yeah?" Bentley waves the waiter over. "We'll have one of each of your desserts."

The waiter's eyes widen. "Sir, we have eleven different desserts, including four cheesecakes."

"Even better," Bentley says.

"But she might not even eat them," Barbara says, on a roll. "She's really, really picky about dessert."

"Why?" Bentley asks.

"Because she's an epically good pastry chef," Barbara says. "Duh."

"Wait, you are?" Dave asks. "You said you were 'decent at cooking.'" He makes air quotes, as if that shows how much I downplayed it.

"She went to the CIA to learn." Barbara snorts.

I need a muzzle for her.

"She's a pastry spy?" Dave's smirk annoys me.

"The Culinary Institute of America's in the city," Bentley says before I can explain. "You went there?"

"On weekends," I say. "Yes."

"And that fancy place in Paris." Barbara snaps. "The schnitzel place. What's it called?"

"Wait," Bentley says slowly. "You went to the Cordon Bleu?"

"Just for six months," I say. "I was obsessed with crêpes and galettes."

The desserts arrive then, and the waiter has to clear everything off the table just to squeeze them all on it.

"So you're like that guy in the rat movie?" Dave asks. "If you don't like something, do you not swallow?"

I laugh. "I'm not as bad as Anton Ego," I say.

"That's her favorite movie, though," Barbara says. "She watched it over and over and over until we all hated it."

"It's hilarious," I say, "but it also has a touching

story to share."

"It's all about found family," Dave says, "and also about chasing your dreams."

"Don't leave us hanging here." Bentley points. "Tell us which of these are good and why."

"What if they aren't good?" I ask.

"Then tell us that, too," Dave says. "Do you think we want to eat bad cake?"

"I watched you eat an entire box of Girl Scout cookies last week," Bentley says.

"Some of those are really good." For some reason, I feel compelled to defend Dave.

Bentley leans a little closer, his mock whisper still plenty loud. "They were expired."

It's clear that these two have been friends for a long time. "How about this?" I offer. "If I find anything truly disgusting, I'll be sure to eat it all so you don't have to."

"Hey," Dave says. "Why do I not trust you anymore?"

"You can't trust her around dessert," Barbara says. "She'll poke your hand to steal the last bite."

Bentley spreads his hands. "You taste all of these, and whichever one is objectively the best, I'll order four more of it. How's that?"

I glance around at the contenders.

Of course, at an Italian place, there's tiramisu. I try not to cringe. "No one around here ever gets tiramisu right. I'll decline to taste it."

"Wait," Dave says. "How do you know this isn't the exception?"

I point. "First, the mascarpone was whipped too long. Instead of being creamy, the fat solidified. You can tell by how it looks right there." I gesture. "And secondly, whoever made this didn't combine the yolks and the sugar fast enough, so the sugar started to dehydrate the yolk, making clumps." I shudder. "Pass."

"Impressive," Bentley says. "I feel like I'm on an episode of *Chopped*."

"She never watches cooking shows," Barbara says. "She thinks they're tiring."

"I couldn't watch *The Apprentice* either," Bentley says. "I get it."

"Wait, what do you do, exactly?" I ask.

"We've all been trying to figure that out for a long time," Dave says. "Best we can understand, he buys companies and either sells the parts, or the ones he doesn't buy, he charges them a bunch of money to fix them."

Bentley looks up at the ceiling. "I just fix them, like a mechanic with a car. I've been thinking of changing jobs to one where I buy them and sell them off. It's riskier, but there's a lot more money in it. Like parting a car for the value of the pieces instead of the whole thing, which might chronically break down and requires ongoing repairs and maintenance."

"So you'd be, like, the chop shop of the business world?" I ask.

Bentley's laugh is low. "I'm going to have to use that."

"With whom?" Dave asks.

"The people who keep offering me a job, of course."

"Alright, what's next?" Barbara asks. "Because I really want that cheesecake."

"This plain one was overmixed," I say. "So there was too much air, and that caused cracks."

"Is that why that happens?" Dave asks. "My mom's

always has cracks."

"Yep," I say. "But that turtle one looks alright." I spear a bite and pop it in my mouth.

All three of them watch me like hopeful teenagers at their first movie audition.

"The flavor's good," I say. "Someone opened the oven while baking it, so that's why it sank here, but it tastes fine."

"I want it," Barbara says.

"Go ahead." I wave her on.

One thing I'll give my friend. She does not eat like a bird. For a thin woman, she puts the sweet stuff away.

"The caramel cheesecake looks perfect." I take a bite, and it tastes a little too eggy. I sigh. "It's alright, but they added too many eggs, or they didn't have the right size eggs. For a commercial operation, it shouldn't happen. They should weigh them."

"And what about all these?" Dave waves at the left side of the table.

"We still have a chocolate mousse cake, a molten chocolate cake, and a chocolate cookie in a pan," I say.

"Okay," Dave says. "Which first?"

"The cookie's overcooked." I slide it away. "The molten cake will be fine—they always are." I take a bite and bob my head. "It's a teensy bit overcooked too, but I don't fault them for that. If they undershoot and it's raw, it's a disaster. The flavor isn't too strong, and they didn't dilute with milk chocolate, so that's a plus."

"And the mousse?"

I debate about this, but finally, I shake my head. "Someone else will have to try it. I'm not a big fan of chocolate, and that's just too much."

"Wait, but you liked the molten chocolate, or at least you didn't complain," Dave says.

"I've learned to eat it," I say. "But milk chocolate is the worst. I just can't."

"I'll take one for the team," Barbara says, snagging it now that she's finished the turtle cheesecake. She tries a bite and beams. "It's even better. I should have taken this instead."

"Feel free," Dave says.

"The cannoli's decent," I say, "but it's clearly been sitting in the fridge all day. Maybe two. That makes the pastry a little soggy and the cream a little congealed."

"And the shortcake?" Bentley looks hopeful.

"They went with a sponge cake," I say, "which is probably the safest, but it's also my least favorite." I point. "And they used a cooked sauce, which, this time of year, why not go fresh?"

"You weren't kidding," Dave says. "She's rough."

I tap the crème brûlée and scoop up a bite. "They miraculously managed to cook it close to evenly, even in this pan that's too tall, but the caramelized sugar to creme ratio is off. They need different ramekins."

"Oh, man," Bentley says. "You know too much."

I laugh. "But I hope I saved the best for last." I shift the key lime cheesecake closer. "I love fruit desserts, but they have shorter shelf lives, usually. For that reason, restaurants often have menus that are heavily skewed toward chocolate and cream-based options."

"But?" Dave asks. "I sense a but coming."

"Key lime pie's often too tart," I say. "Some people like that, but most people find it overwhelming." I pick up the last clean fork from the pile and slide it into the edge. "The most important part about making it a key lime *cheesecake* is that the cream from the cheesecake should counteract the tartness from the lime." I put the bite in my mouth.

And then I close my eyes.

Not much has made me really happy in the past year or so, but this does. A perfect dessert, perfectly executed.

"I think we have a winner, folks," Bentley says.

"Yes." I open my eyes and smile. "We do."

Bentley waves the waiter over. "We'll take three more of those."

Barbara burps. "Just two." She giggles.

"Two," Dave says.

"I won't be able to finish this one," I say.

"You can take it home," Bentley says. "Maybe you'll want the rest tomorrow."

"She has Cheerios for breakfast, usually." Dave smirks.

I remember the Cheerio stuck to my face the morning we met, and heat rises in my cheeks. "Not usually," I say. "Though I do love breakfast cereal."

"Me too," Bentley says. "My favorite's Lucky Charms."

"Too many marshmallows," I say.

As Dave says the same thing.

"That was weird," Bentley says. "Like you two rehearsed it."

"We did," I say. "I prepped him for that before we left."

"But we haven't worked in the bit about the hotdogs yet," Dave says.

"What?" Barbara's totally lost.

"He's kidding," I say.

"You're so funny," Barbara says.

"She's really smart," I say. "I'm not kidding. A little drunk's just not her most flattering look."

"Not everyone went to Cornell," Barbara says, "but I can still count better than you."

Oookay. "You sure can."

"You went to Cornell?" Dave asks. "Really?"

"My parents weren't keen on the chef thing," I say. "It's not really a job with a ton of high-earning positions."

"You clearly love it, though," Bentley says. "Where are you working now?"

"She can't find a job," Barbara says. "Not since she got out of that mental hospital."

I stand up and grab my purse. "I think I'd better get her home." Luckily, Barbara follows me pretty easily. We're waiting for the valet when Bentley stops me.

It gave me a few moments to think of what to say, at least. "The thing is—"

"Here." He hands me a to-go box with my cheese-cake, and starts back inside. But before he reaches the door, he turns. "You don't owe me any kind of explanation. I think you were really brave even to come out tonight."

Brave. That's what you tell kids who try the neighbor's weird casserole without crying. Or the baby who pets the dog with a trembling hand. "Thanks."

"I—" Bentley swallows. "I know tonight probably felt a little bumpy, but I had a great time. I'd love to see you again." He pauses, his eyes full of. . .something. "I'll be in touch."

That was about the opposite of what I expected.

Sometimes surprises can be nice.

6

DAVE

Seren told me her best friend was beautiful, smart, capable, and fun. Usually if even one of those things is true with a setup, I'm over the moon, but Barbara was all of those things.

And I didn't even care.

Because she was sitting next to Seren, who shines like the Hope diamond. Like a Waterford crystal chandelier with two-hundred-watt bulbs. Like Yankee Stadium during the last game of the World Series.

I can lie to myself about all kinds of things, but setting Seren right next to another, perfectly lovely woman? It's painfully clear that stupid Bernie was right—I think I do want to date her. From the second they leave, I can't think about anything but whether she liked the rich, brilliant, well-spoken friend I stupidly just set her up with. The one who *doesn't* compulsively make jokes whenever he's uncomfortable. The one who *didn't* sit, frozen, at the table after her friend said she'd been in a mental hospital.

I googled her, after the Suit made me feel dumb at that meeting.

Before, I had left it alone for the sake of decency. I wouldn't want people learning about me online. But I knew Bentley would look into her—he always does—so I didn't want to be unprepared.

Still, I couldn't believe what I saw.

Her parents.

Her grandmother.

Her sister, brother-in-law, and brother.

Her sister's twin sons.

And her husband of only six months.

All dead within a week of the accident. Two died immediately. I'm not sure what's harder. Finding out they're gone. . .or watching them slip away. Of course, if the articles I found are right, she was unconscious for at least part of that time.

And I made a joke about it.

She should've slapped me. Or cried. Or, I don't know, stormed out. But instead, she laughed. How brave do you have to be to *laugh* in that circumstance? Or, like me, maybe she's a nervous laugher.

Did I just ruin her night?

I think back to a few days ago, when she laughed at my first cringey joke. She hadn't seemed uncomfortable then. She seemed relieved.

By the time I get home, I can't just leave it alone. I have to know if she's upset with me. I text her. SO HOW BAD WAS IT, ON A SCALE OF BAWLING ALL THROUGH DINNER TO BORING ENOUGH TO DRY THE PAINT ON YOUR WALL?

Then I wait.

Ten seconds. Thirty. A minute.

I start to pace in my apartment, genuinely frustrated with myself. Why didn't I wait until tomorrow?

71

Why did I have to text her so quickly after that train wreck? She *ran away* with her friend, for heaven's sake.

But then my phone chimes, and I rush to grab it off my nightstand.

It's not her.

It's Bentley.

I'M GOING TO SEND HER A KEY LIME CHEESECAKE FROM A FEW DIFFERENT PLACES. THEN I CAN TEXT AND ASK HER WHICH SHE LIKED BEST.

I want to throw my phone.

Why did I set him up with her? Obviously Seren's not ready to date. I never should have suggested it. You don't try to use a shovel five minutes after gluing the handle, and I haven't even glued her back yet.

I messed this up.

Plus, based on what I know of Bentley, he should have liked Barbara. She's smart, runs her own business, and she's perfectly curvy. But how could anyone like Barbara—nice, sweet, perfectly wonderful Barbara— when a supernova like Seren's in the room?

I collapse backward on my bed and groan.

I should let it go, but I'm unable to do it. I never let anything go. Before I have time to think about it, I fire off another text.

This one's to Bentley, at least. DUDE, CALM DOWN. YOU DON'T WANT TO SCARE HER OFF, RIGHT?

YOU THINK THAT WOULD?

FOR SURE.

He doesn't text me back, so I just have to hope he's going to listen. It's not like I'm being selfish or something. I thought they might hit it off, but clearly I have more work to do before Seren's ready for anything like that. It's not actually very late, but if I want to wake up in time to work out before I meet the contractors at Seren's tomorrow, I should get to bed soon. Which is why I'm lying in bed in the dark, my phone plugged in across the room so I can stop obsessing, trying to go to sleep, when it happens again.

My phone chimes.

That stupid, awful, horrible, taunting *bing* sound.

It's probably Bentley, telling me he's already spent more money than I spent on my unimpressive, should-be-valeted car, sending the best cheesecake from all of New York City to Seren. It's possible she'd think it was a sweet gesture, but that thought doesn't make me feel better. Probably because I'm worried it'll upset her.

But then I realize something.

He can't do it without me giving him the green light, because he doesn't have her address. Although, he knows her grandma's name. I'm sure he could track down the address for her estate online if he's creative enough. He is very, very creative. I swear under my breath.

And now I can't *not* look at my phone.

I hop up, pad across the carpet of my room, and swipe it open.

IT WASN'T THAT BAD. IT'S PROBABLY GOOD THAT I WENT OUT. UNLESS YOU NOW WANT TO RETHINK BEING MY PARTNER. I WOUDLN'T BLAME YOU.

WHY?

BARBARA WAS DRUNK, BUT WHAT SHE SAID IS TRUE. I'M UNEMPLOYED. . . AND I RAGED OUT ON MY BOSS. I WAS STUCK IN A PSYCH WARD FOR A MONTH FOR BEING A

DANGER TO MYSELF AND OTHERS, IN THE OPINION OF THE STATE OF NEW YORK.

My heart breaks for her.

After what she went through, who wouldn't need some therapy?

DON'T WORRY. MY TAKEAWAY FROM TONIGHT IS THAT OUR B&B IS GOING TO HAVE THE BEST FOOD IN THE ENTIRE CITY. I'M MORE EXCITED THAN EVER.

Minutes pass and she doesn't reply, but for some reason, I'm not ready to let the connection go. I probably just want to feel like I made some progress tonight. YOU SHOULDN'T FEEL BAD ABOUT BEING IN A HOSPITAL FOR A MONTH.

I want her to open up and *that's* what I decided to send? It looks like I'm lecturing her.

But it is true.

MY AUNT WENT TO ONE FOR A WHILE, AND IT SAVED HER. YOU WOULDN'T FEEL BAD ABOUT BEING IN THE HOSPITAL FOR A BROKEN LEG. THIS IS THE SAME AS THAT. YOUR MENTAL HEALTH IS IMPORTANT AND AFTER WHAT HAPPENED, OF COURSE YOU NEEDED SOME HELP.

Still nothing from her. No shock. I sound like Dr. Phil. I slap my own face. With as good as I am at fixing gadgets, who knew people would be so much harder?

I'm about to put my phone in a lock box and walk away when it chimes again.

DID YOU LIKE BARBARA?

That's not the response I expected. How do I answer that? It's a landmine, any way I look at it. If I say I didn't, I'm a jerk and she'll proceed to tell me how great her friend is. If I say yes—for some reason I'd rather die than lie to her about that.

Okay, maybe not *die*. I really need to be more careful about what I'm saying. I had no idea I used the word die so often until I went into business with someone whose entire family died recently.

But it's been an eternity in 'text time.' I have to respond with something. LIKE HER. . .AS A LOCAL BUSINESS MANAGER? AS A RUNNER? OR AS A FUTURE MRS. FANSEE?

ANY OF THE THREE?

SHE WAS VERY NICE. There. That's diplomatic.

SHE'S BEAUTIFUL. "NICE" IS WHAT GUYS SAY ABOUT UNATTRACTIVE GIRLS.

SHE'S NOT UNATTRACTIVE, BUT SHE'S NOT THE ONE WHO'S GOING TO CHANGE MY MIND.

CHANGE YOUR MIND?

How do I respond to that? I never should have texted her in the first place. This was all a huge mistake.

And now she's calling me.

I have to pick up. We've been texting. She knows I'm awake. If I don't pick up, she'll think I'm dodging her calls. Or worse.

Pooping.

I groan and swipe. "Hello?"

"Hey," she says. "I figured it might be easier to call."

Easier. Ha!

"What does that mean, change your mind?"

"Oh, nothing."

"About what?"

She's like my parents' dog Charlie. Once he thinks something is there, he will never stop digging. "I'm just not in a hurry to get married, that's all."

"But what is your mind made up about?"

I collapse on my back on my bed. "I want a few more years of fun before I surrender," I say.

"Surrender?" Now she sounds annoyed. "Is marriage an attack?"

"No," I say. "But once you get married, and you have kids, the fun is over, right?"

"I suppose it depends on what kind of *fun* you're talking about." Yeah. She's royally ticked off.

"You can't go out to eat every night, or go drinking with your friends, or spend an entire day hiking in the Catskills."

"You spend the entire day hiking now?"

"No," I say. "But I *could*."

She laughs.

"What?"

"Nothing."

"What are you laughing for?"

"Do you spend every night out drinking with friends?"

"No," I say. "But if I wanted to, I could."

"So your life isn't that exciting, but you're still too selfish to give it up."

"Look," I say. "This is why I didn't want to elaborate."

"No, I think it's good for me to find out," she says. "I'm glad you don't like Barbara. Anyone who sees marriage as the end of life is too stupid for me to set up with my friends."

"You said she's your only friend."

"My only close friend." Seren huffs.

76

"Listen, I didn't want to pick a fight, okay? But my dad says that one day, I'll meet someone for whom settling down doesn't seem so bad."

"*Doesn't seem so bad*. You're a real gem," Seren says. "A prince among men."

"Okay." I exhale. "I get it. That's fine."

"Is that what your friend Bentley thinks, too?"

I sit up. "Huh?"

"Does he ascribe to the 'marriage is the end of everything' mentality?"

I've never talked to him about it, but probably. Most men do, I think. Seeing as he wanted to send her a thousand dollars' worth of cheesecakes, I doubt he wants me to throw him under the bus. But I can't help myself. Inexplicably, I can't stand the idea of her thinking of Bentley as being *delighted* at the prospect of marriage.

"Of course he does."

"Then I'll delete his number."

"Wait," I say. "When did you get his number?"

"Barbara was telling her story about the flamingos. He wrote my name on a napkin and handed me a pen. Then he texted me right after I left."

"What?" How cheesy is that? What is Bentley, twelve years old? "I can't believe you gave it to him. You barely know him."

"He's my business partner's best friend. Should I not trust *you*?"

My hand tightens on my phone. "It's just that. . ."

What? It's what? I can't really tell her that I think she's not ready to date. I can't say that I need to make a plan to fix her before she can get out there. Or that I want to keep her for myself. . .

"Is there something wrong with him?" she asks.

Something wrong? Lots of things. He's sinfully rich. He's arrogantly handsome. He's so smart he can do complicated math functions in his head. And he *likes* to work out.

"Dave?"

"He usually falls hard, and then once the girl definitely likes him, he'll just change his mind." I wince. "I've seen him do it over and over." I should never have said that. I mean, he likes her enough to send her a dozen lime cheesecakes. He's clearly interested, but the lie just comes out of nowhere.

"Oh."

"Why'd you say 'oh'?"

"He asked for my address," she says. "I just gave it to him a few moments ago. He's not, like, wanted for any crimes or anything, is he?"

Shoot. He's going to do it. He's going to send her a bunch of stuff. And that will make her think about him all the time.

"You should tell him you didn't like him," I say. "I just thought he'd be a good first date back. You know, no sobbing through dinner or painfully boring conversations."

"Okay."

It's quiet, but through the phone, I hear the doorbell chime.

Why's her doorbell chiming? What's going on?

"Hey, Dave, there's someone here. I better go."

It's nine-thirty at night. Who's at her house at *nine-thirty* at night?

"I'll see you tomorrow, right? You're going to be here when the contractors come to give us bids?"

"Yes," I say. "For sure."

"About that." I hear her open the door and say hello.

And then I hear a guy's voice. "Hope this is okay."

Bentley.

It's freaking Bentley.

He's at her house, right now. He's probably carrying fancy lime cheesecake with both hands. What is wrong with him? Can't he listen to the person who introduced him to her?

Before I can make any sense of it, I'm up, dressing, and throwing clothes into a suitcase. What's wrong with me? Why do I care that Bentley's there? He heard about Seren's past, same as me. He can clearly tell she's broken.

Right?

He won't push things too hard or too fast?

Seren needs to slowly get back to normal. Having work to do every day will help, and going on a few dates a month with a new—not as amazing as Bentley —guy each time will help. Slowly, she'll learn to be a normal, healthy, happy person again, a person with purpose. A person with hope.

What she does *not* need is some hot and cold guy chasing her.

Which is why I'm almost to her house, with a suitcase and an air mattress. With contractors coming and going, and soon, work crews, there shouldn't really be a single woman staying there alone. Any of them could notice and come back after hours.

It's not safe.

That's why I'm driving over in the middle of the night to move in with her.

It's not because Bentley's there.

My phone starts ringing just as I pull up. . .and

then drive through the open front gate. It's just hanging open, like a huge blinking light. *Come in and rob me! I'm all alone.*

"Hello?"

"Hey," my sister says.

For some reason, I just assumed it would be Seren. What normal person calls someone just before ten o'clock, assuming they'll be awake?

"Hey, Danika," I say.

"Whatcha doing?"

I'm not about to tell her that I'm storming the front door of my new business partner's house because Bentley's way too interested in her. That sounds. . .I don't know. But not good.

"I'm about to go to bed," I say.

"Aww man, really?"

"What's wrong?"

"I was hoping you'd be in the city, living it up like a single guy does."

"I'm not," I say. "I'm about to go to bed." Only, I'm now parked in front of the house I officially own half of, and I'm whispering. "Sorry."

"Maybe you want to go into town?"

"What do you want?"

"It's not me," she says. "*The baby* wants Rice to Riches."

If she tells me what the baby wants one more time. . . "Have Peter go get it for you," I say.

Her voice takes on the little-sister-whine. "But he's out of town."

"So Grubhub, then."

"You know how I feel about them," she says.

"Because one time they refused to cancel your order."

80

"They kept my seventy-four dollars," she says. "The restaurant didn't keep it. Where do you think it went? They pocketed it, and then they wouldn't even let me talk to a—"

"Dave?" Seren's standing in the doorway of her house, surrounded by a halo of light. She already looks beautiful, but now she looks like an angel.

"I have to go." I hang up on Danika. I'm going to pay for that later. "Hey there."

"Why are you here?" Her eyes shift behind me and widen. "And why do you have a suitcase?"

"Dave?" Bentley's now standing behind her, his head towering over hers almost proprietarily.

I've never in my life wanted to punch my best friend more than I do right now. "What are *you* doing here?" I ask. "It's late."

"Bro." Bentley smiles.

"Is it that woman?" Seren asks. "Does she know where you live?"

I blink.

"There's this crazy person who keeps calling him, and he keeps blocking her, but she won't give up." Seren's eyes are wide. "I've been worried about it ever since I heard that call."

"Yes," I say. "Her. She knows where I live."

Bentley frowns.

"But also, starting tomorrow morning, there are going to be contractors in and out of here at all hours," I say. "I realized that as I heard Bentley just show up."

"You heard?" Bentley blinks. "How did you hear?"

I grab the handle on my suitcase and jog up the steps. "Seren and I were on the phone when you rang the bell."

Bentley frowns. "Is there—"

"We both have to be up early for work," I say. "You probably ought to go."

I keep walking, and Seren and Bentley have no choice but to move out of the way.

"I don't have a guest bedroom," Seren says. "I'm not sure—"

"Don't worry," I say. "I brought an air mattress."

"She has a gated property," Bentley says. "I'm sure it'll be fine."

I fold my arms. "Every contractor and sub we hire is about to have the code, and when I got here, the gate was just hanging open."

Seren's brow furrows.

"Actually," Bentley says, "I think Dave's right. Maybe it is a good idea to have him here."

"Wait, really?" I ask.

Bentley shrugs. "There are going to be a lot of men coming and going soon." He smiles a possessive smile. "I'll sleep better knowing someone's keeping an eye on you when I can't."

Seren looks annoyed by both of us, like we're equally ridiculous. "You need to get a court order against that woman, and then you can go back home." She crosses the family room to the kitchen and closes the lid on a box. "But, oh. Wait. Dave, did you want some key lime cheesecake? Bentley brought me *two*." She doesn't look annoyed, but she sounds. . .brusque?

"I'm not hungry," I say. "We just had dinner."

Seren smiles. "That's what I said."

"But you did try them both." Bentley walks into the kitchen, too. "And you said this one was the best."

"It's Cheesecake Factory," she says. "It's kind of what they do."

"Still," Bentley says. "It's good to know. Maybe tomorrow I can bring some from—"

Seren's shaking her head vehemently, but she's grinning. "No way. Give me time to get rid of these first."

"That's the point," Bentley says. "If I bring more while you still have these, you can compare them better."

They're staring at each other and smiling like idiots, and I want to punch my hand through the wall. "Alright." I clap. "I'm exhausted. I'd better go fill up my air mattress and get ready to sleep."

Bentley lifts one eyebrow like he thinks I've gone crazy.

"You know I can't sleep when there's any other noise," I say.

"You slept through frat parties," Bentley says. "And that one time, when we were in Boston—"

I hold up my hand. "That was a long time ago. Now, I can't sleep when there's even the slightest noise."

"It was so nice of you to bring these." Seren slides the first box and then the second into the fridge. "But I probably ought to go to sleep. Dave's right. The first contractor will be here at seven-thirty."

"Alright, well, I'll call you tomorrow," Bentley says.

After he finally leaves, Seren shakes her head. "It's a good thing you warned me," she says.

"About?"

"Him coming on strong."

"Right."

"If you hadn't, I'd probably think he really liked me." She points at the hallway to the right. "You can take any of those rooms over there. I sleep in the master, as you probably recall."

"Right."

"Do you think staying here while we remodel will be enough?" she asks.

To get away from my annoying but harmless stalker. The stalker I've never liked as much as I do right now. "I hope so," I say. "But I guess we'll have to see."

I absolutely loathe air mattresses, but right now, with her smiling at me, I decide it's worth it.

7

SEREN

Growing up as the youngest of three kids, I was always surrounded by noise. My mother loved to sing. My father's nearly tone deaf, but he liked to recite poems. My older brother listened to rock music around the clock, whether he was working out or working on homework. My older sister was a huge reader, and she always recited things out loud while she worked. We either lived with my grandmother, next door to her, or around the corner, so she was often around too, sharing her thoughts or old stories.

When I moved into my college dorm, my extroverted roommate always had people around, so it was never quiet. And then after I married Will, both of us had big families, so we had what felt like a revolving door on our apartment.

One of the hardest things after the Accident is the silence. There could be no better barometer of how my life changed than the utter quiet I'm wrapped in from dawn to dusk and beyond.

No yammering nephews.

No bickering siblings.

No brother-in-law or husband debating sports nonsense.

No bubbly grandmother.

No humming mother or prattling father.

Just me.

All alone.

Forever.

Sometimes when the quiet encircles me, it feels palpable, like a blanket or a mantle through which I can't breathe. It's as suffocating as a dense scarf, weighing me down with its emptiness. Pressing my heart flat with its bleakness. Dampening any burgeoning hope before it can even try to rise.

As great as my friends are, Barbara and Corey can't break the silence.

Corey already thinks I'm insane for going into business with Dave, so if he finds out that Dave's *moved in* with me, without an invite, without a warning, without a *bed*, he's sure to lose it. I can almost hear Corey in my head, ranting.

But it feels like a weight that I didn't even realize was crushing my chest has been lifted. It feels like, for the first time in over a year, I can breathe freely. I should probably ask Dave to get out as soon as possible, but I can't do it.

I'm so happy not to be alone.

I hope he's a slob. I hope he's noisy and raucous. I hope he eats all my food, and uses all my towels, and doesn't do the laundry. Because that will remind me that there are others in this orbit around me that has been vacant and empty and so desperately lonely that it feels like I'm constantly drowning. The more obnoxious he is, the less alone I will feel.

It's air in a vacuum.

It's light in the abyss.

It's a rope in the depths of despair.

When I go to bed, for the first time in a long time, it's not with tears drying on my cheeks, or with a desperate sob that's not even stifled—because who would hear it, anyway? When I go to sleep tonight, it's with the comforting knowledge that there's a well-intentioned stranger snoring softly in the next room.

The next morning, I slide a bit further into the insanity. Dave's still asleep, and even when I'm the only one awake, my heart races a little at the thought that there's someone here. Someone to cook for. I pop up and dress quickly, and then I scan the contents of my fridge and pantry.

It's disappointing.

Other than the two cheesecakes, there's very, very little.

I've been eating only what was necessary, and it shows. Other than the usual dry ingredients, I only have: an apple, ten eggs, a cucumber, some squash, a few slices of cheese, and half a package of puff pastry in my freezer. I don't eat meat, but I don't mind eggs from free-range hens from farms I've looked into. We used to keep chickens here, but after the accident, I rehomed them. It was too much responsibility for me at the time. I suddenly miss Cluckers, Rose, and Henrietta, the three we had most recently.

Before it even occurs to me how crazy it is, I've carved an apple into a rose and turned that into an apple tart, made biscuits, poached two eggs, and I'm blending hollandaise sauce. The sound of the blender's what wakes him up, I think. Which means he's not a heavy sleeper, but based on the fact that the dings and whisking didn't wake him, he's not light either.

"Seren?" When Dave's head pokes around the edge of his bedroom door, his hair's rucked up on one side into a point, like half of a flock-of-seagulls hairdo.

I can't help laughing.

His frown is even cuter. "What's funny?"

"Nothing." I shake my head.

He sniffs. "Are you cooking?" His eyes swivel until they take in the plates of food. "Why are you cooking?" His eyes widen. "Now I'm going to feel guilty for coming over here."

I shrug. "I like to cook."

He blinks.

"But you don't have to eat it."

He shoots out of his room like he's on the log ride at Disney, minus the water. "You're in luck, because I like to eat." He grins.

"Does that make me Jack Sprat?" I ask. "Or the wife?"

"Jack Sprat can eat no fat?" he asks. "Is that what you mean?"

"Right. I like to cook, and you like to eat. So does that make you the wife?"

His brow furrows. "I suppose it does." He picks up a plate. "But don't get any ideas."

I place a biscuit on my plate, slice it in half, and put a cucumber slice on top of each side for crunch. "About marrying you?" I can't help my snort. "You're safe." I show him with mine how to assemble my vegetarian Eggs Benedict, and then I pour the hollandaise on top. "There."

I slice the apple tart in two and hand him half, and

then I pour us each a glass of ice water. "I wasn't really expecting guests, so my options were pretty limited."

"I'll keep my expectations low." He takes a bite of the tart first and his eyes brighten. His shoulders straighten. "Wow. You really can cook."

I barely eat two bites in the time it takes him to eat all of his and reach for another biscuit.

"Is this okay?"

I shrug like I don't care, but it heals something small inside of me to see someone enjoying my food. Not working lately has negatively impacted more than just my pocketbook.

"You may make me rethink the whole *marriage is the end of all good things* party line, if you keep cooking like this."

Before I can object to his 1950s cliché, his phone chimes.

"Oh," he says. "The first contractor's here, waiting outside the gate."

"I have the list of things we discussed," I say. "And the budget you emailed."

"You cook and you're organized?"

"Don't tell Bentley," I say, "or he might regret it when he changes his mind and drops me."

He frowns. "It's not that—"

"I'm kidding. Calm down."

I buzz the gate open, and while we walk to the main house, Dave runs through our primary budget items. "Roof, furnishings, the bathroom and kitchen remodels, and the dining room."

"Right."

"And if we have anything left over, we had lots of ideas for the grounds."

"That's a nice way of saying we don't agree." I arch

one eyebrow. "I still can't believe you want to tear out the entire garden."

"It serves no purpose," Dave says. "It's a waste of space and resources."

"It sets the tone," I say, "from the moment they pull through the gate. It tells them, 'you may have just left the city, and you may yet be in Scarsdale, but for now, you're safe. This is your home away from home.'"

"But they know it's a hotel," he says.

"When I was a kid," I say, "we went on a vacation to Ireland. Most of the places we went were modern and posh." I close my eyes for a moment. "But one place we stayed was called Castle Leslie."

The contractor waves at us.

"The difference between an inn and a hotel is that personal touch," I say. "The *feeling* that being there brings. You wanted my grandmother's home for exactly that reason, and the garden is what truly sells it."

"Did your castle have a big garden?" Dave arches one eyebrow.

"Of course it did. When we reached Castle Leslie, it was like driving into a park. The bucolic setting, the lush greenery, it reminded me of the place I'd always loved most." I drop my voice as we approach the contractor. "This estate."

He rolls his eyes, but I hope he at least considers it. "We need more parking, though."

"Right," I say. "I agree. Some of it will have to give way to pavement." I heave a sigh. "But sometimes the obvious value isn't the only value in something."

Or maybe that's a lie I use to excuse the time and space I waste.

The first contractor's horrible. The next one is

even worse. After the third quotes us the highest amount yet and complains nonstop about the changes we want, I'm ready to cry.

"Just one more today," Dave says. "Don't worry. If these are all bad, we'll keep looking."

"It's not so much that they're awful," I say. "It just costs so much more than I thought, and none of them seem *excited* about it." Actually, it didn't even feel like they were really listening.

Until Luis shows up, in an old white pickup truck that backfires a lot. He has a paint smear on his temple and crinkle lines around his eyes, and I love him from the first moment. "What a gorgeous garden." He looks around and inhales slowly, and then he exhales just as thoughtfully. "It feels like a place to just. . .reset. In the middle of the city."

"An oasis," I say. "That's the word you're looking for."

He smiles and nods. "It is. *Sí.*"

As we walk the kitchen, and he suggests opening up the room so that it's visible from the dining area, Dave and I freeze. "But we want them separate. It's an inn."

"You said it's more of a bed and breakfast style, no? It's in vogue right now for the people working to be seen and to see the people they're working for. They can see the fresh ingredients you're using, and aren't you going to be cooking a lot of the time?" He catches Dave's eye.

I'm not sure why.

Luis shrugs. "It can't hurt the ambiance." He winks at me.

And I blush.

"You do look just like your grandmother," Dave

says. "He's right. We'd be stupid not to capitalize on it a bit."

"I like the idea of wallpaper in these bathrooms," Luis says.

"The other contractors said that was an unnecessary expense," I say.

Luis frowns. "Unnecessary? You wanted a vintage look. Nothing says vintage like a classy paper. Floral prints, probably, to go with the baroque theme?"

"Country meets baroque," I say. "Not a lot of gilt and enamel or anything."

"How does a contractor like you know what fits with baroque?" Dave asks.

"I graduated with a degree in art." Luis grins a sideways smile. "Any idea what people who graduate with art degrees do?"

I shake my head.

"Me neither. So I became a painter. Something I could use my color sense for *and* still pay my rent."

Dave laughs.

But as we work our way through the home, he continues to make sensible suggestions, including things I'd never have thought of without his advice. "You can save a bundle and keep things on point with used toilets and tubs. My wife refinishes old tubs and they're beautiful. And much more cost effective." He points at the budget. "You could trim here, and have more here." He points at the wallpaper.

I can't help meeting Dave's eyes, which are dancing, as we reach the end of the upstairs hall. He and I are nodding, and I know we're on the same page.

"What about that?" Luis looks up at the pull cable for the attic.

"Just the attic," I say. "There's a partially finished

room we used to play in, but it's only nice enough weather to use it about half the year, and we can't really send guests up and down a ladder."

"I'd love to see it anyway," he says.

Which is how, for the first time in years, I'm scrambling up a wooden, drop-down ladder to check out a dusty old attic.

"It's massive," Luis says ahead of me. "It runs the entire length of the house."

"Yeah," I agree. "But—"

"Whoa," Dave says, just ahead of me. "What's all this stuff?"

As I step through the doorway into the actual attic, leaving the playroom, I can hardly believe what I'm seeing. Chairs, beds, tables, boxes, and lamps are haphazardly scattered all over the attic storage.

"The estate sales team came through the house and cleared it out," I say. "I guess they didn't think to look beyond the playroom. My grandma liked to redecorate, but whenever she did, she'd keep most of the old stuff she replaced. She couldn't bear to part with it, and she always said you never knew what might circle back around."

Dave looks as delighted as I feel. "I wonder how much we'll be able to save on furnishings with this stuff." He whistles.

And then breaks down into a fit of coughing, thanks to the horrifying level of dust we've kicked up.

"It'll take a little elbow grease," I say. "But I think I have an idea for how to spend our free time for the next few weeks."

❦ 8 ❦

DAVE

Seren must've given Barbara my phone number. She texts me first thing the morning after our date, and even though I'm not responding, she just keeps right on texting.

WHAT DO YOU LIKE FOR BREAKFAST?

I'M HAVING A GREEK YOGURT.

DO YOU WORK OUT? I'M OUT FOR A RUN. I COULD BE RUNNING BY YOUR APART-MENT RIGHT NOW, FOR ALL I KNOW.

Cleary a hint that I should tell her where I live.

I don't mention that I'm eating breakfast made for me by her friend. The one who set us up. My inclina-tion is never to reply at all, but that feels kind of cruel. I doubt it will win me points with Seren, either, so I reply with a simple, ALREADY WORKING.

As I'm walking through the house with contractor number two, I begin to wonder if a brusque response might be worse. Did that give her hope?

"Barbara says you've been texting," Seren says.

One text from me is texting? I decide to change

the subject. "What's in this sandwich?" Seren made us sandwiches, since we only have fifteen minutes until the next contractor shows up. "It's better than anything I've ever had at Subway."

"It's the tapenade," she says.

"What's that?"

"An olive spread," she says. "But you dodged my question."

Not easily misdirected. I'll have to remember that. "Barbara's been texting me." I swivel my phone around so she can see.

She squints, and then she snatches the phone out of my hand.

"*What do you like for breakfast?* was her question?" She raises one eyebrow.

"I couldn't really tell her that I was eating the best Eggs Benedict I'd ever had."

She tilts her head. "Wait, really?"

"I haven't had them very often, but it's true. I thought they were better without the Canadian Bacon, or whatever usually goes on there." I shrug.

"Then Barbara, even though you didn't respond, says, *I'm having a Greek yogurt.* And you still didn't reply."

"What am I supposed to say? That Greek yogurt is gross?"

Seren snort-laughs and then claps her hand over her mouth.

It's the cutest thing I've ever seen.

"Even though you kept ignoring her, she texted *again* to ask if you work out." She compresses her lips. She must be reading the part where Barbara says she could be running by my apartment.

"I shouldn't be reading this."

"I replied then," I say. "I didn't want to be rude."

Seren scowls, so somehow that was wrong, I'm just not sure what part.

"What? Where did I go wrong?"

"Barbara's a very literal person," she says. "She's a runner. She's a business manager. And she clearly likes you."

I swipe my phone back, my fingers flying over the keys. I HAD A GREAT TIME AT DINNER, BUT I DON'T THINK THAT YOU AND I ARE A GOOD FIT. I WISH YOU WELL. I swivel it back around. "How's that? Clear enough?"

Seren scowls.

I'm getting colder, clearly. "What's wrong now?"

"She likes you," she says. "She's trying."

"You can't magic a person into liking someone back," I say. "And while I thought she was perfectly nice, she wasn't right *for me*."

She rolls her eyes. "You didn't give her enough time to really find out."

"I don't need more time," I say. "You say she's literal? Well, I'm decisive. I can look at something or someone and decide without wasting time whether it's a fit. Barbara's very nice, but she's like a dryer sheet. She clings to me too hard. It's off-putting."

"That's rude and unfair," Seren says. "A few easy-breezy texts doesn't make her clingy."

"I said I liked ice cream," I say. "She started telling me how much she'd been craving ice cream. I told her I enjoyed looking at art in museums and she started telling me her favorite paintings. When I said I liked to go jogging, she texted me to say she was running. . .maybe by my apartment."

"So you like a lot of the same things," Seren says. "That's good, right?"

"It feels like she's saying she likes everything I like."

"But—"

"It's true that I'm busy with a project right now." And no one will be the right person while I'm trying to help Seren get back on track.

"So am I," she says. "Hello—partners. But I'm finding time to text Bentley back, and politely too. And I'm talking to Barbara about why you don't seem interested, which would be way easier if you'd take thirty seconds and be a little more invested."

"So she did notice I wasn't very responsive," I say. "That might make this message overkill." But I press the button and send the text anyway. "Because now, at least no one can accuse me of wasting her time."

"I guess we won't be doubling anymore." She pulls out her phone and starts typing.

"Wait, who are you messaging?"

"Bentley," she says. "Who else?"

"You're still talking to him?" I slide my phone into my pocket and clench my fist. "Why? I told you how he is."

"He's bringing more cheesecakes by later." Her sideways grin irritates me. "He's pretty funny, you know, even if he is going to dump me as soon as he thinks I like him back."

Bentley is many things. Smart. Rich. Savage, even. But funny isn't one of them. "No, he's not."

"He is." She's *still* smiling. "He just said that once we pick a number one lime cheesecake, we should branch out." She looks up, her eyes alight. "For research purposes, you know."

"How is that research?" I ask. "Cheesecake isn't something people eat for breakfast. We won't be serving anything but breakfast, right?"

She frowns. "That's a good point."

"Unless you *want* to serve desserts." I mean, it's her specialty, right?

"I love to cook most anything, but I became a pastry chef because we almost never have to work with meat."

"Ah," I say. "That makes sense. Do you hate cooking bacon, then?"

She shrugs. "I don't love it."

"So we won't have any meat products," I say. "It's not like you *have* to offer that for breakfast."

"I don't ask people to give things up for me," she says. "My family never stopped eating meat, and I wouldn't dare ask Barbara not to drink, for instance."

"But you'd rather not cook it."

"They have some decent substitutes, or if you were around, you could cook the bacon," she says.

A strange vision flashes in front of my eyes. Me in an apron. Her, effortlessly whisking eggs. Both of us laughing. Customers ordering things. Bumping into one another while carrying trays with orange juice on them.

I shake my head. "You don't want me cooking bacon. Trust me. I burn most everything."

She laughs. "Meatless options it is."

Later in the day, we discover a treasure trove of furniture and belongings. We also sign a contract with a contractor we both love. We don't even have to talk it over. I can tell right away that she likes Luis, and he's the first person who seems both cost-conscious

98

and hard-working. The fact that he's got an artist's eye is a bonus.

After our new contractor leaves, Seren starts back up the stairs toward the attic.

"You're going up there again now?" It's already five o'clock.

"Bentley's not coming until seven," she says. "I figured if I have some time, I may as well use it."

I grit my teeth. I'm heartily sick of hearing my buddy's name coming from her mouth. "I can help."

"I'm sure you have better things to do," she says.

It occurs to me for the first time that she may not *want* all the things upstairs to be used wherever possible for the inn. "We don't have to use that stuff for the guest rooms, you know."

"Huh?" She turns back to gape at me. "I thought—"

"I mean, that's not part of our partnership agreement. You own all of it. You could sell it. You could keep it." I shrug. "Either way, I'm still happy to help. I'll haul it all down. But you can do whatever you want with it once it's down here and cleaned up."

Her face falls.

Why did that make her sad?

"I contributed the estate," she says, "and the contents of the attic are part of the estate."

"But you contributed to our partnership, and as a partner, I'm saying we didn't know about those items. They're personal property, as far as I'm concerned."

This time, she smiles. "I appreciate that. I may keep a few things."

"Your house is totally unfurnished, other than that mattress."

"Actually, we haven't talked about how long I can stay there. It's in the partnership agreement that once we're done remodeling the main house, we'll convert the carriage house to a rental area as well."

"It is?" I don't recall seeing that part. "But when we spoke that first day, I said you could stay on property as a caretaker. I'll keep my word."

She's back to looking upset.

"What I mean is that you can just keep living there, for as long as we're running the inn."

"Why would you do that? It's four rooms we could otherwise use to generate income."

"We need you close so you can make epic breakfasts that people will rave about," I say. "So having you onsite makes sense."

She blinks.

"Even long term, it could be one of the perks of the job, living there since you're cooking." I clear my throat. "I think it *should* be one of the perks of the job."

"The contract said I'd be fine through the remodel, and your budget projections included the carriage house rooms, so I thought you'd changed your mind. Which makes sense. It's a business, after all."

"Forget those," I say. "Things always shift a bit in operations, and I've been thinking about it." I hadn't really, not until this moment, but I make decisions quickly. As soon as I said the words, I realized they were true. She grew up in that house, on this estate, and she should stay here as long as she wants.

Fixing something that's broken isn't always about glue and tape. Not with living things, anyway. Sometimes it's about putting it somewhere it can heal with joy. I can tell that this place means a lot to her, and she's going to heal the fastest living here.

"We can circle back around to it later," she says. "You may change your mind. But for now, that's really generous."

As we start sorting through the stuff upstairs, I realize how different her attic is from most people's. My parents' attic, for instance, has boxes with tax files, Christmas decorations, and tons of batting that's probably more of a fire hazard than an insulator.

This attic has paintings, antique furniture, and boxes full of expensive china.

"Why would your grandmother have four enormous sets of china in the attic?" I ask.

"As to the place settings, she entertained a lot. But for the variety, she got sick of things easily." Seren laughs, inhales dust, and starts to cough. "But then, she'd circle back around and want them again ten years later."

"I wonder if we have enough of this—"

"For the breakfast service?" Seren's eyes are twinkling. "I had the same idea. It would really add an air of sophistication, using Royal Crown and Wedgwood china, don't you think?"

"Maybe not for groups with children," I say.

Her eyes soften. "Maybe not, but even kids deserve something nice. You'd be surprised how much more careful most children are when they realize you're using something special."

That's what Seren adds to everything. Just being in her presence makes the day feel special. I'm not shocked to hear that people around her feel it, too. "I must not be special," I say. "Most kids just want to punch me."

"Punch?" Her eyes widen.

I smile. "My nephew's almost three and he punches me every time he sees me. Though, that may have as much to do with the types of games that I suggest as anything else."

"Your nephew?"

"My sister's kid," I say. "And she's about to have another one, heaven help us."

Seren smiles. "How exciting. When's she due?"

"A little less than two months from now, and she knows it," I say. "She keeps calling me and asking me to bring her random things, like super posh rice pudding."

"Rice to Riches?" Her eyes light up. "I love that place."

"We should get some," I say.

She arches one eyebrow. "*We* should?"

"For my sister, I mean."

"You weren't suggesting a date, right?"

I roll my eyes. "I'm not that stupid. But we could grab some for ourselves, together, without it being a date. We're business partners, remember? We're bound to do things together regularly."

"Like eating breakfast. And lunch?"

"Sure."

"And sorting through old furniture."

"That too," I say.

An hour later, Seren checks her watch. "I'd better go down and get cleaned up a bit. Bentley will be here soon."

I'd forgotten about that. Or maybe I suppressed it. "I can't believe you're letting him come over again," I say. "I told you already—"

"That he'll be super interested at first, and then he'll dump me?"

"Right."

She shrugs. "Sounds therapeutic."

"How so?"

"It'll be nice to have an ex who isn't dead."

She's heading down the stairs with a smirk on her face, thinking how she made a macabre joke, totally unaware of how my heart reacted to that statement. I glance around at our piles. She chose about a dozen things we can use in the rooms at the inn. Four or five of those items require small repairs. She also chose some things to haul to the trash. And about eight things we went through, she flagged as items she'd like to keep at the carriage house. I like the percentages. I pick an end table earmarked for her place and carry it down with me.

"What are you doing?" She's looking up at me from the bottom of the stairs.

"I figured I may as well bring a few things down today."

"Oh," she says. "Okay, great."

Once I reach the bottom, she takes the end table from me.

"I can get it," I say.

"So can I," she says. "I'm not broken, you know."

Something about the way she says it makes me think she wouldn't really appreciate me telling her that I'm trying to fix her. It also makes me happy in a way I can't explain.

Probably because the first step in healing is deciding to do it.

I'm not broken sure sounds like someone who wants to heal.

Since she's taking the end table, I head back up and grab a box of china—one of the ones in the set she wanted to keep for herself. She called it Vera Wang Wedgwood Lace, and I approve. It was the classiest looking one. I'd feel terrible, watching customers break it.

"Man, this china's heavy," I say, as I set it carefully on the floor in the kitchen of the carriage house.

"Thanks for bringing that," she says. "I'd probably have dropped it. Or given up on the front porch." Her smile makes it worth the effort.

"I don't really understand why people—women. It's only women—like china, but I'm glad we have it already, since you do."

Seren crouches down and sets her hand on the top of the dusty box. "Wedgwood has a saying, you know. *Your plate is the canvas; the food is the art.*"

I think about that. For a chef, it's probably more true than I realized. "The most complicated thing I ever make is nachos, so maybe that's why it never occurred to me before."

She laughs. "So much of our enjoyment in eating comes from the presentation. China helps enhance that, so it's worth the effort and expense."

"I don't think I've ever actually eaten on china. We're more of a paper-plates-at-all-big-gatherings-to-save-time-on-cleanup kind of family."

"This morning was the first time I've wanted to cook—no, to create art—since the Accident."

When the doorbell rings a second later, I want to punch Bentley in the face. She's finally making progress, talking about cooking and the accident, and he's interrupting. When she hops up, a sparkle in her eyes, to answer the door, I realize something that makes me uncomfortable.

Could her progress be *because* of Bentley?

And more concerning still. . . Why does that idea upset me so much? Shouldn't I just be pleased that she *is* making progress? I mean, there have been plenty of girls I might have wanted to date, but if Bentley had expressed an interest, I'd have backed off, no hard feelings.

Why does this one make me want to attack my best friend?

"Ready?" Bentley's wearing dark jeans and a polo shirt—his *I'm comfortable but still fashionable* outfit. I hate that he's trying so hard with her. He didn't just rush here right after work in a suit. He went home first. Changed. *Then* rushed here.

"Oh." He nods at me. "You're still here."

"I am." I shove my hands in my pockets. "Where are you two going?"

"I told him that my fridge can't hold any more cheesecakes," Seren says. "So he suggested we should go to the restaurants on his list and try them in person. We're starting with Ladurée, off Broadway."

"It's not going to be quite as fair," Bentley says. "We won't be able to compare them in a face-off, but Seren assures me she'll be able to keep them straight."

"We can't all be food connoisseurs," I say.

"But now I have one for myself to guide me." Bentley wraps an arm around Seren's shoulders, and I shoot to my feet.

I type Ladurée into my phone, and I get lucky. "It's on Broadway?"

"Excuse me?" Seren's grabbing her purse.

"The place you're going," I say. "Near Soho?"

Bentley scowls.

"I have to go to Rice to Riches for Danika, remember?"

"Wait, she knows your sister?" Bentley asks.

"Not yet," Seren says. "But we were talking about her pregnancy cravings earlier."

"I told Danika I'd grab her some rice pudding," I say. "And that's right by where you guys are headed. We can share a cab."

"I drove," Bentley says.

"Even better." I smile.

Bentley might be the one to hit me if I keep this up, but Seren seems fine with it. She even ducks into the backseat of the car, gesturing at the front seat of Bentley's Bentley Continental.

"It's too bad your parents didn't name you Jeep," I say.

It's an old running joke.

"Then Seren would have way more room back there."

His Continental GT is fairly spacious for a sporty model, but it's not exactly an SUV.

"You shouldn't let her get back there," Bentley says. "You're the uninvited tagalong."

"She told me to sit here."

"His legs are way longer than mine," Seren says. "Besides, you two know each other way better. It makes sense for me to sit back here."

"That's the point, though," Bentley says. "I'm trying to get to know you. I already know way more than I want to about this loser."

In spite of his grumbling, Bentley's about to put the car into drive when another vehicle pulls up behind us.

"I think that's Corey," Seren says. "Hang on a second."

"Who's Corey?" Bentley asks.

"Her pretentious best friend who's in love with her," I say.

"Pretentious?" Bentley asks. "In love?"

"He's my oldest friend," Seren says. "And he never comes over unless he needs something." She taps the back of my chair.

Part of me wants to refuse to move.

But finally, manners win. I'm grumbling as I climb out of the front seat and flip it forward.

A man's climbing out of the shiny red Range Rover behind us. Why doesn't it surprise me that guy drives a Range Rover? It's as expensive and impractical as a sports car, and it gets just as terrible gas mileage, but it says *I care more about looking tough than going fast.*

There's no way he's ever going to take it off-roading. The roughest terrain he probably sees are the cobbled streets of Cambridge on his visits back to Harvard.

"Serendipity?" Corey asks. Then he winces. "I mean Seren."

"Is everything okay?" She walks toward him. "We didn't have plans, did we?"

"I didn't realize I needed an appointment to see you," he says. "I just came by to check on you. I wanted to see how the partnership's going."

"Great," Seren says. "In fact, we're about to grab some food."

"We?" Corey glances behind her, eyeing the Bentley.

"This is Dave, whom you met before, and that's his

best friend, Bentley Harrison." Seren points to us in turn.

"Wait, Bentley Harrison. . ." Corey frowns. "The newest principal with Bain Capital?"

Bentley smiles. "We should get going. I have a reservation at Balthasar as soon as we're done at Ladurée, and we need to drop Dave off on the way."

"Oh, don't worry about dropping me anywhere. I'm starving, so I can come with you to dinner." It's actually fun to watch the muscles in Bentley's jaw work and the vein in his forehead throb.

"Well, if they have room for three, they have room for four, right?" Corey asks.

"What's going on with you guys?" Seren asks. "Whatever it is, it's getting weird. Corey, I'm doing great, and I'll call you tomorrow."

"I can't come?" Corey asks. "Why? Is it a date?"

"Yes," Bentley says, at the same time that I say, "No."

My best friend glares at me.

I glare right back.

"I'm calling the restaurant," Corey says. "I bet they can seat us all."

"No one has asked me what I want to do," Seren says.

All three of us freeze. We've broken the cardinal rule.

We've pissed off the girl we were trying to impress.

"I'm going back inside." She glares at all three of us.

Corey runs after her.

Lucky guy.

I'm stuck dealing with Bentley, who looks about as angry as Seren.

"Listen," I say.

"No." Bentley shakes his head. "You listen."

I probably deserve that.

"You called to set me up with a woman you're going into business with." Bentley's eyes spark. "A woman so beautiful that you snapped a photo to convince me. And it worked."

"I know. I'm sorry, but—"

"But what?" Bentley slams the door of his car closed. "You set me up, and then you show up and block me last night. And then again today. What's going on?"

"The thing is," I say, "I feel responsible for her."

"Try again."

I clear my throat. "She's really nice, and she's had a rough year, and I want to help her."

He shakes his head. My oldest friend in the entire world shakes his head, but he also starts to smile. "Are you really this stupid?"

"Huh?"

"I've known you for more than twenty-five years, man. I've watched for years and years while everyone underestimated you. I've seen you underestimate yourself. I've watched you take care of your dad's business without making a big deal about it. I've watched you care for your sister. But this is the most irritating of all."

"This. . .what?"

"You're planning to run an inn with a woman you barely know, a woman you keep talking about nonstop."

"But the thing is—"

Bentley slams his hand against the frame of his

beautiful, outrageously expensive car. "You don't even know the thing, so shut up for a minute, dummy."

He's never once called me stupid in our entire friendship. Is he really that angry?

"You've never remembered a girl's name longer than a week. You're dating someone new constantly, and with a face like yours, you get away with it."

A face like what? What's he saying?

"But for the first time, you really like someone. You like her *so* much that you're throwing her at me and then yanking her back like she's a yo-yo."

Throwing her where? A yo-yo?

"I only pursued her so you'd recognize it."

"Recognize. . ."

"I mean, if I'm wrong, I'll gladly march right in there and face off with Mr. Superior who seems to think he has a prior claim. But if I know my best friend Dave *at all*, and I think I do, you'll march in there and take care of that yourself."

Take care of. . . "Wait, you're taking her out because you think *I* like her?"

"I'm taking her out because I think she's lovely, but I'm trying not to get too invested, because yes. I think that the world's least insightful man is *mad* for her. Bernie knows it, and luckily he warned me."

"But she's—"

"Your business partner?" Bentley's smirking. "She's stunning. She's elegant. She's talented. She's smart. Probably too smart for you, but I see geniuses with doofuses all the time. And most of all, she's fragile in a way you have always craved."

"I hardly think—"

"Once you repair her damaged parts," Bentley says, "you'll never let go. And she won't want you to."

"You've misunderstood."

"I haven't," Bentley says. "But you may be too idiotic to realize that what I'm saying is true. That's why I came back today, even though the more time I spend with her, the more *I* like her. I did it to force you to realize how much you like her."

"I don't want to marry anyone," I say. "And I signed an agreement saying we wouldn't date."

"Oh, I know about your stupid fears. You're so afraid that any girl you really like will reject you, that you never date anyone you really like."

"What?" I ask. "That's crazy."

"Ever since Valerie in twelfth grade," Bentley says. "When she left you and started dating that loser Chad, you just quit liking anyone." His smile widens. "And that's how I knew you really liked this one. The more eagerly I pursued her on that date you set up, the more upset you became. Instead of backing down, you doubled down."

"Yeah, but that's because—"

"Normally I'd have just humored you in your lies. I thought we had loads of time. But that guy." Bentley swings his thumb around and points it at the house. "That guy's not going to back down for you. If I had to guess, I'd say he waited a long time for this chance. He liked her before and got friend zoned, and he's been waiting for a suitable amount of time after her accident to try and pursue her. But now he's realized there's blood in the water, and he's not about to let another shark swim by and snatch her up. Not again."

I hate everything he's saying.

And that may be the strongest argument that Bentley's right. But even if he is, that old friend of hers is rich, good-looking in a forgettable way, and he already knows her really well. She barely knows me, and she even put a clause in a contract that I can't date her. If I do, she can immediately kick me to the curb.

She clearly wants nothing to do with me. Now that I think that, I realize how much the thought stings.

❧ 9 ❧

SEREN

For years and years, my one port in every storm has been the same. Corey Fairchild. When I woke up in the hospital after the accident, he was the first person I called. He flew to Florida immediately. Even then, he was solid. Calm. Dependable. I've never even seen him upset.

Until right now.

"I told you there was something strange about that guy." He's pacing in my kitchen. "And now that Bentley guy, too? Do you even know who he is?"

I shake my head. "Do you?"

"They call him The Axe. He's fired more people than anyone else at Bain."

"He's *fired* people?" I'm a little lost.

"Bain's a consulting firm. Their job is to come into companies that are struggling and optimize them so they don't go under."

"And he works for Bain?"

"He's a principal," Corey says. "That basically means that he and a few other guys run the company, and he got there by ruthlessly cutting any segment of their clients' companies that wasn't bringing in enough revenue. Thousands of people lose their jobs every year because of him."

"But you told me that consulting firms help the economy because without them, the struggling companies go under. Then everyone loses their job, right?"

"That's true, in the aggregate, but he's utterly cold-hearted about it."

"Okay, so because he's really good at his job, at paring down the inefficient parts of companies, we hate him?"

Corey frowns. "Actually, I kind of admired him. In a I-wish-I-was-that-cool-but-could-be-nicer-about-it sort of way."

"But now?"

"Now I hate him."

"Why?" I ask.

"Because I don't want you to date him," Corey says.

"Why?" I sound like a broken record.

The front door opens then, but I hardly even register the movement.

"Because I want to date you." Corey swallows hard then, his Adam's apple bobbing. "I've always wanted to date you."

"Always?"

"The day you met Will, at that pool party, I had a whole thing planned." He closes his eyes. "I ordered a huge pizza that said, 'Serendipity, would you date me? Love, Corey.' But in pepperoni."

I remember that day. The day Will told me I made my hot pink bikini look good. I must have blushed as bright as the swimsuit. He asked for my number and had me write it on his forearm, so every other woman there would know he was already taken, he had said.

"No pizza ever came," I say.

"I stopped them when they showed up," Corey says. "I paid them fifty bucks to take it back to their apartment."

"You were going to tell her how you felt with pepperoni?" Dave asks from the front door.

"It's none of your business," Corey says. "Get out."

"Actually, Dave's living here for a while," I say.

"He's *what*?" Corey asks. "You can't be serious. You don't even know him."

"She's a vegetarian," Dave says. "You could have used bell peppers or something."

"Is that really the point right now?" Corey asks.

Dave shrugs and walks the rest of the way inside. Then he shuts the door after him. "I met Seren almost two weeks ago now. I barely know her, but I do know she's vegetarian. I feel like, if you wanted to tell her how you felt, you should've paid more attention."

Corey's entire face turns red. "Listen, I've liked Serendipity for years."

"But you keep calling Seren by the wrong name," Dave says. "People change. You should try to keep up."

"Dave." I inject a note of warning into my voice.

"I'm sorry." Dave holds up his hands. "I'll just duck into my room and let you keep wooing her. It seems to be going really well." He disappears, and I realize that I still have to deal with Corey.

My oldest friend.

Who says he liked me before Will ever asked for my number.

"Why didn't you say anything before?" Every time I open my mouth, more clichés fly out. "Why now?"

"You were happy with Will," he says. "I wanted you to be happy, so I let it go."

"But now?"

"You've been really sad," he says. "Everything I did just made it worse, so I backed off."

"Backed off? You went to Sri Lanka."

"To give you space, but then I came back to see if you were happy to see me."

"I'm always happy to see you."

"I love you, Seren." Corey's looking at me so earnestly that I panic.

"I can't," I say. "I love you, too, but not like this. It feels all weird."

"Because of Will?"

"Because of you," I want to say. But I end up saying, "I don't know."

The blood has drained out of Corey's face, and he stares at me for a moment, and then finally, he leaves, quietly closing the door.

I went from a date at a posh place to a weird confession from an old friend, and I don't love any of it. My carefree night's a wreck, and all I want to do is cry.

So it's like every other night of the past year and change.

I grab a package of Pop Tarts and run back to my room.

The next morning, I wake to the sound of a drill. When I fling my door open, Dave's reattaching a leg to the ottoman we decided would work in the sitting room of the old mansion.

"Wow." I yawn. "Six-seventeen in the morning felt like a good time to be doing that?"

"Since you went to bed at seven-thirty last night, I

figured you'd be fine with it." He smiles and flips his safety glasses up on top of his head. His hair's suitably ruffled thanks to that, and it looks cute. Actually, cute's the wrong word.

Wearing jeans and a grey t-shirt that hugs the muscles in his chest, with messy hair and bright, eager eyes, my partner looks *hot*. Not handsome, or cute.

Definitely hot.

It's probably the first time I've thought that about anyone in a long time. Guilt floods into my chest, crowding out any other feelings.

So I squash the thought, carefully.

"I didn't go to sleep last night at seven-thirty," I say. "I went to hide in my room because everyone in my life had gone insane."

"Well, I went ahead and moved some things from the attic into the spare room here. You can tell me where exactly you want them later. The other stuff, I put in the room next to the attic ladder. I have a list of what we need to make the repairs we've identified, and now that you're awake and suitably annoyed with me, I figure that's my cue to go."

"Go where?" I straighten.

"To Scarsdale Hardware," he says. "To pick up this stuff." He brandishes a list at me, but the only thing I can make out is 'dark stain' and 'wallpaper samples.'

"I'll come," I say. "If you can wait for me to shower."

"It's fine," he says. "I can do this by myself. There's no need to rush."

"If I come along, we can just pick the wallpaper instead of looking at samples."

"That's true," he says. "Alright. I'll wait."

He ends up having to wait a while. After I shower,

I blow dry my hair. Then I flat iron it. I throw on some basic makeup. I change clothes three times.

Finally, I'm ready to go.

For a trip to the hardware store.

Dave doesn't complain, but I wonder what he must be thinking. It's not normal to need over an hour to get ready for the hardware store. "Sorry," I say.

"For?"

"Taking so long."

"I would say that beauty takes time, but you looked just as lovely before you fell into that hole in the bathroom."

"So you did notice that it took a long time."

Dave shrugs. "I have a mother and a sister. An hour's not really that long."

That makes me laugh. I don't imagine my brother would have been so magnanimous about it. "Sorry about the awkward scene last night. I probably should have handled it all a lot better. Is Bentley upset?"

At least Dave doesn't seem angry as he gestures at the door to his Honda Accord, telling me he'll drive.

"Bentley is. . .Bentley. He never gets upset."

"He got stood up on a date we made plans for, because my friend showed up and threw a fit."

"That wasn't your fault."

I'm still too scared to even check my phone and see who has called or texted. I'm not sure I can deal with any more nonsense from Corey.

"Are you alright?"

"As alright as I ever am." I'm not trying to sound depressed, but as usual, my joke comes out a little too close to Eeyore. Self-effacing jokes worked better when everyone didn't chronically feel sorry for me.

"Your friend Corey threw a lot at you last night," Dave says.

"Apparently I've been a little obtuse." I still have trouble believing he liked me for all these years. Why didn't he say something before now?

"It's not on you, that you had no idea he liked you, you know."

"Well."

"I knew how he felt about you the moment we met." Dave's eyes are on the road, but he's smiling.

"You did? How?"

"Have you ever seen a dog mark its territory?" His eyes are merry. "They circle and pee. Then they walk around a little more and pee again. A few moments later, they do the same thing. He did the human equivalent that day at the lawyer's office. He was throwing out 'mines' and wrapping his arms around you, and referring to your shared history over and over."

"So I am an idiot," I say. "And I should have noticed."

"Only other dogs notice when a male dog's marking his territory." Dave's smile is bemused.

Wait. Does that mean. . .?

Dave clears his throat.

"So you're saying that you noticed. . .because—"

"Corey felt threatened by me," Dave says.

"But you don't even want to get married." I laugh. "I can't think of anyone who should be less threatening to him. You even set me up with your friend, which is who my date was with."

Dave looks pretty uncomfortable, but luckily, we've reached the hardware store, and he pulls into a spot and opens the door. Without saying another word about the Corey-Bentley mess, we're suddenly marching inside and picking out varnish, stain, wallpaper, and light fixtures.

"Luis sent us that text about those supplies we need to select, too," Dave says. "I figure we may as well grab that stuff while we're here."

"What about the business account?" I ask.

"I have the credit card linked to it," he says.

"But some of those things are for my place."

"You can pay for those," he says sensibly.

"Duh."

We're nearly to the register to pay when Corey calls. I stare at the name on the caller ID like I suddenly don't read English, unsure how to react.

"If you're scared to talk to him, that's your answer," Dave says smugly.

"Maybe not," I say. "I mean, sometimes it takes time to think things through."

"Not things like this." Dave looks far too pleased with himself, and that bugs me.

So before the call goes to voicemail, I swipe. Now at least Dave's not beaming anymore, but I still have no idea what to say to Corey.

"Hello?"

"Listen, I'm not calling about last night, though I'm relieved you didn't screen my call. I just wanted to tell you that our firm has a new client, and that client's son has a restaurant in Scarsdale, and it's a long story, but I found you a job if you want it. They need a pastry chef ASAP, and they have a Michelin star, so it's got to be someone epic. I told them you were the best I'd ever seen and then some."

Talk about pressure. "I'm more of a pie and cake at a diner kind of—"

"Stop," he says. "You and I both know that's not true."

"Corey, I—"

"If you turn this down because of me, you're an idiot, and we both know you're not that." He sighs. "I'm going to text you the information. Pick up the guy's call."

"I'm renovating an inn that I'm going to run. I don't have time for a new job."

"Tell me you're sure that inn thing is going to work, and I'll tell him never mind," Corey says. "But I think you'd be wise to find something that will provide a consistent income."

He hangs up, but I can tell that Dave followed our conversation just fine.

"Prince Charming offering you a white horse?"

"Sort of," I say. "His client needs a pastry chef."

"And he happens to know an excellent one."

"Or a mediocre one, anyway."

"You need to stop selling yourself short," Dave says. "I had the breakfast you whipped up with whatever was in your fridge, and I'm sure you're better than mediocre."

"Either way."

"If you want to take that job, I can handle things with the remodel. You can do both for a while—keep your options open."

"That's hardly fair, since we're partners," I say. "I can't expect you to do the majority of the work while I spend all day elsewhere."

He shrugs. "I expect you to do all the cooking once it opens." He smiles. "But that's more because you're a woman, and that's a woman's job."

I roll my eyes.

"Hey," Dave says, catching the attention of an employee. "Do you have any idea where the hose attachments are? You know, like the spray nozzles?"

"They're out in the gardening section. It's outdoors," the short man says.

"And will we be able to check out with all this stuff out there?"

"Sure," he says. "Same as any other register."

"Thanks." I start pushing the cart in that direction.

"Luis said we need to have a place for them to spray things off, and we thought that big drain out back would work."

"On the corner of the patio?"

Dave nods.

"I'm going to look at these plants," I say. "You can pick the sprayer and meet me at the register?"

Dave and I split off, and I push the cart down the first aisle with flowers. I used to spend hours each summer out with my grandmother in her gardens. She had two paid gardeners, but she liked to work on things herself. It was the biggest thing she and my mom—her daughter-in-law—had in common.

Grandma's the one who told me, when I asked why she didn't just let the gardeners do everything, "No one else cares for the things we love quite as well as we do ourselves."

That line has stuck with me my whole life.

She's right, of course. The things we love are always cultivated the best by us. No one being paid for the work will care quite as much. But ever since that day, the things I love have been gone.

It's not just that they all died.

The other things I loved died with them.

I stopped caring about plants, about gardens,

about cooking, about everything else. Because all of it reminded me of them. But that meant that instead of just losing them, I lost it all. Everything that brought me joy was just gone all at once.

I reach out slowly and touch the tough, maple-shaped leaves of the flowering raspberry. People don't usually care much for these bushes once they discover that their berries aren't the ones we're used to buying on the grocery aisle, but birds love them, and their blooms are lovely. Before I have time to think much about it, or how Dave wants to rip the overgrown gardens out entirely, I lug two big buckets into the edge of our cart.

"You like those?" a kid asks.

My head snaps sideways.

He looks like he's an early teen maybe, with dark brown, nearly black hair and honey-brown eyes. He's holding a leaf blower under one arm, and a drill under the other.

It's a lot of weight for a little kid to be carrying.

"These?" I point at the blooming raspberry plants.

He nods.

"The birds love the berries, and I like the smell of the flowers."

"So you know they aren't regular berries."

I nod slowly. "I'm more surprised that you do. Most people see raspberries on the tag and assume it's the kind they buy in stores."

"My mom loved plants," he says, "but we liked the bearberry better."

"This one?" I point at the dark-green-leaved perennial. "The deer love the berries, but we don't get many deer in the middle of the city."

"Birds eat them, and so do rabbits. And they form

123

in the fall, when most critters don't have much else to eat. And in the spring they get little pink flowers. See?" He points at a tiny flower hiding behind a bunch of leaves.

"I do."

"You should take one of these. They'll even grow in rocks."

"Will they?"

"I like things that still grow in weird places," he says.

Something buzzes in his pocket, probably his phone, and he snaps to attention. "I've got to go."

"Okay." I point at the bearberry plant. "I think you sold me on it, though. I'll take one."

He sets the drill and the leaf blower down and picks up the pot that has the single pink, bell-shaped flower. "Here?" He points at the empty corner on the edge of the cart.

"Thanks."

He grabs his boxes again and jogs away, his baggy pants sagging as he walks.

What a sweet kid.

Only then does it hit me what words he used. His mom *loved*. They liked. . . My heart contracts. Does she not love the bearberry plants anymore? Or did she pass away? I never know whether to ask, and I'm someone who has lost people, too.

"What are all those?" Dave's striding toward me down the aisle. "I thought you wanted a plant or two for inside your house."

"I loved these two as a kid." I point at the ones I grabbed. "They smell great when they bloom, which look." I point at the buds forming. "It's about to happen. Plus, the butterflies love them."

"What plant is it?" he asks.

"It's a purple blooming raspberry."

"The pastry chef's buying raspberry bushes?" He shrugs. "You had me at raspberry."

"Not that kind."

He frowns. "What other kind is there?"

I flip the tag over and show him the photo. "They're not raspberries like you're used to, but birds love the little berries, and the blooms smell great. They'll keep weeds away, too."

He rolls his eyes.

"And this one." I point at the bearberry. "I wasn't even going to get this one, but the cutest little teenage boy just convinced me."

"You're kidding me. A cute teenager? I'm pretty sure that's an oxymoron."

I laugh. "But he really was. He was all helpful, and he acted like it was his job to convince me to try the bearberry."

"Another berry we won't eat, I take it?"

"But the birds love them too, or so he assures me."

Dave looks up at the ceiling and shakes his head with a half-smile on his face. "Heaven help me."

"I'll pay for them."

"You should spend your money on something that will actually make real fruit." He reaches for the cart to push it for me.

"Just because it's not what you're used to, that doesn't mean it has no value." I shove past him, not letting him take my cart. What if he tries to evict my three *useless* plants?

We're waiting in line at the checkout, next up to pay, when a kid shoots past us with his arms full. He's carrying a bunch of things, and dread steals through me. It's a leaf blower, and drill, and a bag of something.

There's a car idling up ahead, and the checker picks up her phone. It all happens so fast that I have trouble processing it. "Hey," the checker says. "I've got a runner. License number XCT889. Blue Ford Focus. Old. Bad paint."

The kid yanks the door to the car open and starts throwing things in. First the long box, then the drill, and finally, the bag of whatever.

"What's going on?" Dave asks. "Is that kid stealing?"

"It happens all the time," the checker says. "They'll catch him before they get out of the parking lot."

My heart breaks a little bit.

When it first came out, I felt a bit bad cheering for the thief in the *Tangled* movie. But as the movie went on, I found myself solidly in his corner. And now here I am again. That sweet, helpful, optimistic kid is stealing.

And they're positive he'll be caught.

"What if I pay for his stuff?" I blurt.

"Huh?" The checker turns slowly. "Do you know him?"

I deflate a bit. "Not really, but he helped me pick this plant, and he put it in my cart for me. He's polite, and he's really young."

"A polite thief?" The woman rolls her eyes.

Sure enough, the car's only a few hundred feet away when the police show up. They block the car. The checker's ringing up our last items when the police walk inside, dragging the boy and a very surly looking woman behind them.

"I need a statement," the policeman says. He bobs his head.

His partner drags the kid toward us. "Is this the boy you saw?"

"What's going to happen to him?" I ask.

Dave shushes me.

I'm not sure why, but I'm panicking. *His mother loved plants.*

"His mom'll go to jail," the officer says. "But he's young. I'm sure he'll just get juvie."

"She's not my mom," the kid says, glaring.

Of course she's not.

I can't watch them handcuff him or drag him off. I just can't.

"I'll pay for it all," I say again. "Maybe it was a misunderstanding."

"Was this lady involved?" the officer asks, looking at the checker.

She frowns. "I don't think so. She just feels bad for him. The kid talked to her."

"I'll need your statement too," the officer says.

I fold my arms. "No."

"Excuse me?" The officer steps toward me, his chest puffed out. "Lady, you don't get to tell me no."

"I think she does," Dave says. "You can't just walk around dictating to average, law-abiding citizens." He holds up his index finger. "And I'd like to see a manager. If we pay for these items, we'd like to know whether this will go away."

"He ran out the store," the officer says. "He didn't pay then, and you can't pay for it now."

"Unless the store disagrees," Dave says.

I'm proud of him in that moment, almost unbearably proud. He was embarrassed of me at first, I could tell. But now that the police are here, now that the kid's in the thick of it, Dave's got my back.

You don't find out who someone really is until things go wrong.

Apparently we're both the kind of people who side with a thief.

"It's fine," the boy says. "I don't know them, and they don't know me." He shakes his head. "You don't have to pay for anything."

"See?" the checker says. "Just some lady he talked to." She hits a button on the register and it bings. "That'll be seven hundred and thirty-two dollars."

A drill might be a few hundred. A leaf blower, too. But I bet we're about to spend the same or more than what that kid just tried to steal. Only he's going to juvie, and we're just going to walk out.

Once Dave pays, he's ready to leave.

"I can't," I whisper. "I can't leave until I know what happens to him."

Dave doesn't argue. He just nods. "I'll get this loaded and come back."

So we sit and wait for the manager.

When he finally comes, he looks supremely annoyed. "Why do I have to come down here for a shoplifting charge?"

The police point at me. "She's insisting."

I spring to my feet. "Can you consider letting this one go?" I inhale. "I'll pay for the goods."

"Do you know the boy?" The manager tilts his head. "Is he your kid?"

I want to say yes. I want to step in for him, but I can't. I don't even know his name. "No." I start to cry.

It's so embarrassing.

This happened in school, too. I'm not much of a

public speaker, and when things get stressful, I cry. I swipe at the tears. "He's not my kid, and he's not your kid, but he's *someone's* kid. And if he *were* your kid, would you want him to go to juvie? Did you even ask why he stole that stuff?"

"Look lady, do you know how many Karens come in here every day? Complaining about their paint color. Complaining about some kind of ad copy. Upset that we have men who look like men on our banners." The manager shakes his head. "I can't handle any more hippies today." He walks off.

"Wait," I say. "So will you still press charges if I pay for the goods?"

He ignores me.

"They always press charges," the police say. "It's their store policy."

A sour-faced woman in a grey suit walks through the door from the main store. "I'm Alice Keys. I'm here for the kid."

"The kid?" I perk up. "Why are you here for him?"

"I'm his caseworker." She pulls a piece of paper out of her bag and offers it to the police officer. "It's his first count."

"That we know of," the policeman says.

"Sure," Alice says. "And that means it's still the first."

"Wait. Why does he have a caseworker?" I ask.

"They assign all us us one." He sounds unimpressed.

"Emerson Duplessis, age thirteen," Alice says.

Emerson. I roll the word around in my mouth. I like it.

I like him.

Actually, I want to roll him up and tuck him under

my arm. Then I want to walk away and hug him for hours and hours. I'm guessing I can't do that. So I keep standing here.

"Where are his guardians?" I ask.

Emerson's holding a clipboard the officer handed him, looking at some piece of paper.

"He doesn't have any," Alice says. "He lives in a group home."

"A group. . .why?" I ask.

"Why?" Now she looks like she wants to slap me. "Because there ain't enough foster homes in the area, alright? Who are you? Mary Poppins?"

I ignore her rudeness, focusing on the relevant material I've learned. "Does that mean he has no parents at all? He just lives in a house with a bunch of other kids?"

"You're correct that he has no parents." She frowns and puts her hand on her hip. "Listen, this ain't a new problem, okay? It's just new to you. And if you heard about some shoplifter on the news, you'd be outraged and want them to press charges. So just go home, and let us do our jobs."

"No." I frown. "Emerson, don't sign anything they hand you, do you hear me?"

"You can't tell him anything, lady," the officer says. "For the last time, butt out."

"Oh, I think I can advise him, since no one else is. I'm going to be his foster mom." He seems like a sweet kid. They don't have enough foster parents. How hard can it be?

Poor Emerson drops the clipboard, his mouth dangling open, his eyes widening even more.

DAVE

Once, when I was thirteen years old, I had a test in math. . .a test I was *not* ready to take. I didn't cheat, even though I could have. I didn't copy the rules on my hand or slide a cheat sheet under my desk like my friends did. I didn't even try to sneak a peek off my neighbor's test.

But I did bomb it, utterly and completely.

When the teacher passed out the grades, she would usually mention who got the highest one. Sometimes she'd also mention the lowest. She felt it helped encourage kids to excel, and discourage them from being unprepared.

When she announced that I scored forty-two points on that test, the meanest kid in our class, who also happened to be the richest and the best-looking, said, "Garbage guy's got garbage brains."

Sadly, the name grew even more popular.

When kids started chanting it in the cafeteria at lunch, none of my friends did a thing about it, except for Bernie and Bentley. They told everyone to shut up.

When that didn't work, they hid in the library with me.

None of the teachers did a thing.

As an adult now, that might be my biggest disappointment. You expect adults to be, well, brave. Strong. Smart. Kind. All the things we're taught we should be. But adults are just like teenagers, only bigger, and usually even more afraid.

So when I walk back to the hardware store, and I hear Seren say she's going to be that kid's foster mom.

. .

I should be horrified.

Seren can barely keep her own life together. She's in no place to be fostering a kid. But he's essentially standing in a cafeteria, and the people he thought might help him, his advocate, the police, the woman who's already in the back of the cop car for stealing, are all looking away. . .

Seren didn't.

She may not be able to do as much as she'd like.

But even having someone to hide in the library with you can be huge. I'm really, really proud of her in that moment. For standing up. For trying to do something.

"We both will," I say.

"Excuse me," the woman in the grey suit says. "But who are you?"

"He's my business partner," Seren says. "We jointly own an inn. It's opening in two months."

"An inn?" The woman frowns. "Do either of you have a stable home or the time to become a foster parent? I've been a caseworker for fourteen years, so believe me when I say that becoming a foster parent's not a formality. It's a lot of work. These kids need stability and—"

"I'll do it." Seren swivels her phone around. "I looked it up. I imagine since you're insisting on pressing charges, he'll be put in juvenile detention pending the results, which I'll be very interested in following."

"That's true," the caseworker says.

"And I'll get approved before he is released, so when he's ready to come home, he can come live with me."

"You're, what? Twenty years old?" the caseworker asks.

"Twenty-seven," Seren says. "And four months."

I can't help laughing.

"Is this a joke to you?" The angry caseworker rounds on me. "She's proposing that she foster a kid who would have been born when she was fourteen years old. Does that seem humorous to you? Because it does to me, and that's a problem."

"I don't find that funny," I say. "It's your reactions that are making me laugh. Seren's completely serious, and if that kid had any idea what an amazing chef she was, he'd be even more excited."

"You think his problems are about whether he *eats well*?" she snaps. "Is this something you're doing on a whim to feel like a good person?"

"Am I doing it on a whim?" Seren shrugs. "Yes, but it's a good whim, and I'm not doing it to feel better. I'm doing it because it's the right thing to do." She presses her lips together. "You're asking questions of the wrong person, though." She turns toward the boy. "Emerson, do you *want* a foster home, or would you rather stay in your group home?"

He blinks.

"Because if you have friends that feel like family there, or if the people who run it are good people you'd like to stay with, I wouldn't dream of ripping you away. But I do think it would be nice to hear what your mom did with bearberries when I plant the one I bought today."

Emerson swallows. "I'd like to come live with you." Tears well up in his eyes. He scowls and wipes at them. "If you need help with the plants, I mean. I'm good at stuff like that."

The angry woman rolls her eyes. "That's a terrible reason to have a foster kid."

"It's better than taking one to qualify for a check from the state," I say.

She sighs. "At least that's a reason that will last."

Of course, that's when another man arrives, ready to relieve the officers of custody of Emerson.

"Wait," Seren says. "Let me give you this." She hands a piece of paper to Emerson. "If you have a phone or something, put my number in. You'll have your own room at my house, and we're not that far from here. I live in Scarsdale."

"Okay." Emerson takes the number and tucks it in his pocket.

"Feel free to text or call me whenever you're allowed. And I won't plant the bearberry until we can get you to my house and let you pick a place." Her smile's like a sunrise.

The teenager nods.

Seren doesn't stop watching until he's in the car and it drops out of sight.

"That's a pretty big thing to decide at the hardware store," I say.

She shrugs.

On the drive home, I keep waiting for her to say something, but she just stares out the window. We're pulling into the garage—she gave me a clicker to the garage doors that open onto the street this morning—when she finally speaks.

"Do you think I'm an idiot?"

"What?" I put the car in park and turn. "No."

"I can't even take care of myself." She sniffs.

"You can, and you are."

"You know what I mean." She looks down at her feet.

"Seren, I think you'd make an excellent foster parent for that kid."

"I would? Or I will?"

I could kick myself. I should have said will. "Will," I say. "I hope it all works out."

"You're just saying that."

I drop my hand on her arm, lightly. "I'm not."

She turns toward me then. "You said you'd help."

I shrug. "I will."

"I don't think you should."

It feels like she slapped me.

"It's not that I'm saying you wouldn't be good at it," she says softly. "But you said that getting married feels like the end of your life, like everything you enjoy will just wither away. This is a bigger deal than that."

"Right," I say. "Yeah."

"And maybe, if he's going to come live with me, you should move out." She turns soulful eyes up at me. "Before he moves in."

It makes sense. She's not being rude. I only showed up to make sure she wasn't all alone while people were coming and going, and allegedly to get away from a girl who never even reached out again. "Let's contact social services today and find out what you need to do and how to get things lined up."

"I'm not sure they let you pick a foster kid," Seren says, her jaw jutting out a bit. "But I mean to try."

I imagine the system's overwhelmed enough that they'll let someone amazing like Seren do most anything.

The next few weeks almost prove me wrong.

First comes the initiation of the home study. That's hard enough to line up. Also, the state training and criminal background checks are their own kind of nightmare. References, of which I'm proud to be one, aren't too bad, but they take time. And finally, Seren only lacks the home study itself.

Part of me thought that maybe her enthusiasm would fade while dealing with all the red tape, but it doesn't. Not a bit.

We spend most days meeting with contractors and answering their questions, reviewing brochures, and interviewing possible staff. Seren and I fall into a sort of pattern. She handles most of the administrative and management stuff, and I obsess over the budget and argue with contractors about timing and cost.

She selects what she likes best for linens, sends me options, and I tell her which are within our budget parameters. She chooses from there, and we order them. We select things like wallpaper and tile together.

We spend most every evening working on cleaning, restoring, and repairing furniture, decor, and other things we bring down from the attic. It's not enough to furnish all the rooms of the inn, but it's a decent start. And it's all free, since Seren's not charging the partnership for any of the things she chooses not to keep. We've both gotten pretty handy with glue, screws, and paint.

I discover that Seren looks *adorable* with paint on her nose.

Today, they're installing the toilets and shower drains and sinks in all the bathrooms. . .and the woman who's handling Seren's home study is coming tomorrow.

Which means she's a complete mess.

"You'll be out by tomorrow, right?" It's the fourth time she's asked me.

In the last hour.

"Yes," I say. "Bentley's coming to help me move things into the truck in ten minutes."

The partnership now owns a white pickup truck. It seemed like a wise purchase, especially since we have plenty of paved parking now, and most places charge an arm and a leg for delivery.

"Okay."

She's said okay four times, now, too.

"Maybe you should run to the grocery store," I say. "You never know what kind of cereal he might like. Having a few options—healthy ones—might be a good call."

Her eyes widen. "Do you think so?" She hops up and grabs her purse.

"Seren."

She freezes.

"I'm kidding. You never even eat breakfast cereal, except as a dessert late at night, and you already bought six boxes."

She scowls at me. "That's not funny."

"Right." I shake my head. "Of course it's not." I

lean against the wall. "I'm just trying to calm you down a little. When that lady comes out in the morning, she's going to be bowled over by you. You've got this beautiful house—"

"Full of old, weird, hand-me-down furniture."

"Family furniture that your grandmother collected." I look around the room, stopping at the elegant chaise lounge. "Your grandfather bought that for your epically famous grandmother while they were in Paris together."

"It's hardly practical."

"And that sofa." I point at the light blue corduroy sofa. It's positioned in front of the television, which I brought over from my apartment. "It may not be a brilliant color for toddlers, but you don't have any. And it's exceptionally comfortable."

"It's the sofa Grandmother had on set when she filmed *Moonlight Garden*."

"You said," I say. "But your grandfather thought it looked terrible with his leather wingbacks, so it went up to the attic."

Seren nods. "Wish I had those wingbacks. They were nice."

"You need to stop fretting about everything and find your inner peace. You've gotten a call every week from Emerson when he's allowed to use the phone, and he's still excited to be placed here, with you."

She nods.

"Your home study's going to be amazing, and they're going to love you."

A few moments later, Bentley knocks on the door.

"And now my friend's here to help me move my stuff back to my place, so there's nothing that might stand in your way." I yank the door open.

Bentley's wearing an immaculately matched Adidas workout ensemble, complete with striped pants, a coordinated t-shirt, and a striped jacket. Late spring in New York isn't exactly cold, but it's still brisk after the sun goes down. He's not improperly dressed. It's just a little too much.

As usual.

"Ready to sweat?" I ask. "Because your outfit looks prepped by a stylist for a commercial."

Bentley rolls his eyes. "And yours looks prepped by a blind person."

I glance down at my blue t-shirt and jeans. "It's fine."

"Yeah, what's wrong with his shirt?" Seren says. "I like it."

"Don't sic your girlfriend on me," Bentley says. "Geez."

"His what?" Seren shakes her head. "Keep messing with me, Bentley, and you'll see what happens to your *outfit*."

After leaving that day, he never called her again—I worried that she might be mad. She just accepted it as being in line with what I told her would happen. But maybe she was a little sore. . .

"I don't want to get in the way," she says. "So I set up an appointment to meet the appliance lady over at the big house. I'll be back in an hour."

"I should be mostly out of here by then," I say. "Want to try and grab dinner to review our list of prep leading up to the soft launch?"

"Sure." Seren grabs her purse. "Metro?"

"We can go over together. I'll be back here in an hour or so." It makes me nervous when she takes the subway alone, not that I'd tell her that.

"Okay, if you want." She shuts the door behind her.

"You're going to cry," Bentley says.

"What?" I head into my room. "When am I going to cry?"

"When you have to go back to your apartment tonight." Bentley smirks. "All alone."

"Shut up." I pick up one end of my mattress.

Bentley sits down on a chair.

"That's not even mine," I say. "It's staying here."

"You idiot."

I roll my eyes. "Did you come to help me, or not?"

"Not." Bentley folds his arms. "You love this girl. It's in every line of your body. You turn toward her every time she's in the room. You laugh at all her jokes, even the stupid ones. You talk about her incessantly, and you agree with everything she says."

"None of that is true."

"You love her." Bentley stands up. "You should not be moving out."

"You're just lazy," I say. "I'll call Bernie."

Bentley snatches my phone out of my hand. "Why won't you admit it? Just to me."

"Fine." I try to grab my phone back, but he's too fast. "What if I do? She doesn't like me, not like that."

"You told her, and she said that?" Bentley asks.

I huff.

"You're just scared," Bentley says. "But you're not the garbage guy. You never were."

"Shut up," I say.

"You're running an inn. The Colburn Inn, grace personified."

"I said to shut up."

Bentley hands me my phone. "You may not want to hear it, though why not, I will never understand, but you let those guys get to you back then. You never let go of that, and now, you're letting it wreck your life. You're valuable for more than just fixing things up. I just hope you realize it before it's too late, before someone who *isn't* your best friend, someone who won't beg off out of courtesy, comes along and snatches that girl right out from under your nose."

Bentley turns around and walks out the bedroom door, not helping me move a single thing.

I rush after him, but he's already headed for the front door.

"At least help me move." I reach the entryway just as he's opening it. "You said you would. I can't carry that bed myself."

"I'll help once you admit you love her—to her—and tell me what she said." He swings the door open.

And there's a very shocked, very stuffy looking woman right outside.

"Oh." Bentley says. "Who are you?"

"I'm Mrs. Barrett," she says. "I'm here for a home study for Mrs. Colburn."

"That's not right," I say. "That's tomorrow."

"It's most certainly today." She flips a paper over on her pad. "It says right here."

"But Seren thinks you're coming tomorrow," I say. "We're not quite ready for you yet."

"We?" Mrs. Barrett asks. "According to my notes, there's only one resident of this abode, and her name is Serendipity Colburn."

"She goes by Seren," Bentley says. "And this is her boyfriend, David Fansee."

Mrs. Barrett starts to jot down some notes.

I groan. "No, no, I'm not her boyfriend, and I don't live here. I mean, I have been living here, but I'm supposed to be gone by the home study. See, we work together—we own that inn out there. We're getting it ready to launch in a few weeks, and it was easier for me to be on site. But now that it's opening, and she's going to foster Emerson, we're—I'm—leaving. Going back to my apartment, which I've always had."

Mrs. Barrett tilts her head and squints her eyes at me. "Okay."

"Right. So, see? Maybe you can come back tomorrow."

"Young man, I already moved things around to expedite this. After today, my next opening is six weeks from now, on the eighth of June."

"Oh, no," I say. "No, no, we need to get this home study done."

"We?" She arches one imperious eyebrow. "I thought you said it was only her?"

Bentley laughs.

"You, go get Seren." I bark the order. When Bentley doesn't move, I add, "Now."

"Me?" Mrs. Barrett asks.

"I'm pretty sure he means me," Bentley says. "I'll be right back."

Bentley may think I'm not the garbage guy anymore, but here I am, wrecking Seren's life just like a garbage guy would.

❧ 11 ❧

SEREN

Bentley's arrival in the middle of my meeting can't be anything good. Did Dave hurt himself? Did he bump a pipe while moving and now we've got an active leak in the middle of the bathroom?

That's totally how my life goes.

"Is Dave okay?"

"He's fine." Bentley winces a bit. "But there's been a scheduling mix-up, I think. There's a woman there named Mrs. Barrett. She says she's supposed to be conducting a home study." He clears his throat. "Right now."

I shoot to my feet. "I'm going to have to reschedule with you." I grab my purse and the materials Melinda brought. "I'm so sorry."

"Home study?" the appliance rep asks.

I nod.

"Good luck," she says. "Adoption is the best."

"Oh, she's not adopting," Bentley says. "She's fostering."

But as I walk away, it occurs to me to wonder why

I feel so drawn to this, but I hadn't even considered adopting him. Should I adopt Emerson? I could be his actual mother. . . So what if I'm only fourteen years older than him?

Or is that insane?

I'm practically jogging by the time I reach the carriage house, and I'm definitely winded. I should try to find time for some kind of cardio. Not running—I hate that—but something. There's cardio that's not running, right? I add it to my mental list to find out what other options I have. It would be terrible if I just fell down dead from a heart attack because I'm so monumentally out of shape.

But finally, I reach the front door and fling the door open.

"Okay, how about this one," Dave's saying. "Do you know why seagulls don't fly over the bay?"

Mrs. Barrett shakes her head.

"Because then they'd be bay gulls." He laughs.

Mrs. Barrett does not.

"Oookay," I say. "Thanks for keeping her entertained, Dave, but why don't you head back to your place now?"

"I heard he lives here." Mrs. Barrett crosses her arms.

I swallow. "I mean, he did, but he's moving out."

"But as of today, the date of the home study, he's living here. Right?"

Ugh. "Yes, I mean, he is still here, but—"

"We frown on people changing things around just for the home study," Mrs. Barrett says. "Usually those types of things revert as soon as the child's in the home."

"But his residence here was always temporary," I

144

say. "He moved in because he had a—" It might not sound good if she thinks he has a stalker. I mean, stalkers can be dangerous, right? So that's not a great reason to give. I swallow. "He moved in so it would be easier to meet with all the people who were coming and going with the inn, and so he'd rest easier, knowing none of them would think I was living here alone."

"Not that she's not capable of living alone," Dave says. "She's more than capable, and she had been living here for a long time, all by herself, and she was just fine. Just like she will be when Emerson comes."

"You know, there's nothing wrong with having a live-in boyfriend," Mrs. Barrett says. "But we will need to do full criminal checks and background checks on him."

I sigh. "You may not believe me, but we really aren't even dating. We're business partners."

She looks irritated. "The man who left to get you said he was your boyfriend."

What's she talking about? Bentley? Why would he say that? I shake my head. "He must have been making a joke."

But we're clearly not off to a good start, and this matters to me. I need to fix it. I have to fix it.

"Here, let me show you the room Emerson will have."

"Is it the same room that this guy's vacating?" Mrs. Barrett purses her lips.

"No," I say, "but see? You must believe that he's not my boyfriend, because he had his own room!"

Bentley finally reaches the house and just barges right in, like he's also living here. He looks around, his eyes widening as he takes in the mood.

Mrs. Barrett sighs. "One of the most important parts of a home study is the faith I have in you as an honest and upright person."

"I am honest," I say. "Dave's not my boyfriend. He's my business partner."

"That's entirely true," Bentley says. "I could testify to that at court. I was joking before."

"Can you two just leave?" I ask. "You can come back later to move this stuff out."

Thankfully, Bentley and Dave don't argue. They just go.

"Let's chat," Mrs. Barrett says.

I follow her into the family room, and she asks me a very long list of questions. Most of them are pretty routine, like, 'Where do you work?'

I explain that I don't really have a job, per se. I'm remodeling a house that used to be mine to make it into an inn. But it is an investment that will pay off. I offer to grab the modeling, but she shakes her head.

Then she asks where I sleep, and I show her.

She asks why I want a child to come stay with me.

I explain how I met him, and the connection we forged over a plant that's still sitting outside on the porch, being watered every day, waiting for him to come help me find it a spot.

With each question, Mrs. Barrett makes a soft *hmm* sound and scritches on a pad with her pen. I can't tell if she hates me, disbelieves me, or what.

"Look," I say. "I know this might seem strange. I'm young, I'm single, and I want to foster a child."

"We're nearly through," she says. "Let's just stick to the formal questions."

So we do that. I do my best to stay upbeat, even though it feels like I'm failing completely. It's a strange feeling, inviting someone into your home to evaluate you for a task that you don't really feel qualified to perform at a baseline. . .but that you desperately want to do. It feels like I'm being judged, and I worry that I'll be found wanting.

Every single door that opens reveals something else I can't believe I never noticed before. In the kitchen, my knife block's just resting on the counter, out in the open. In my bedroom, my jewelry box is simply lying, exposed, on the middle of my dresser. I know foster kids have trouble with taking things, and I've taken no steps to help him make good decisions.

Emerson was arrested for theft, for heaven's sake.

Then in the laundry room, there's about a dozen harmful chemicals, all just sitting on an open shelf.

I'm absolutely positive that I've failed when there's a knock on the door. It already feels like things couldn't go worse, but in my life, that's never the case. That's why, when I open the door, I'm not even shocked to see that it's Corey.

He just dropped by in the middle of this.

Because *why not?*

The one person I haven't told about what I'm doing, because I know he'll really think I've gone insane. At first, I didn't use him as a reference because I thought he might be mad I didn't take that pastry chef position. But then I didn't tell him about what I was doing because I didn't have the energy to deal with him objecting.

Now I'm kicking myself for not eliminating that hornet's nest before the inspector came.

Anything in my life that can go wrong, no matter how unlikely, is always bound to happen.

"Corey," I say.

"Is this a bad time?" He frowns. "It looks like you have company."

"Who's this?" Mrs. Barrett asks. "Another boyfriend?"

"*Another boyfriend?*" Corey scowls. "What's going on?"

"I'm a social worker," Mrs. Barrett says. "I'm evaluating Mrs. Colburn to determine whether she's a suitable foster parent for one Emerson Duplessis. He's a thirteen-year-old boy who was recently arrested for shoplifting." She's studying his face. "And who are you?"

Corey looks like a cartoon character who was just smashed in the face with a two-by-four. His eyes are wide and bulging. His mouth is dangling wide open. "She's—what?"

"I'm going to be a foster parent to a kid I met at the hardware store," I say. "He needs someone. Right now he's stuck in a group home."

"I hope that right now he's in juvie," Corey says. "Geez, Serendipity. I mean, I know things have been rough since the accident, but is this really what you think you should be doing? When you don't even have time for an amazing job I found, you want to, what? Adopt a troubled kid?"

"What accident?" Mrs. Barrett asks.

"Oh." Corey looks like he just realized we're not alone.

I close my eyes.

"What accident are you referring to, sir?" she asks again.

"I'd probably better come back another time." Corey ducks back through the door and shuts it.

"My father was driving," I say. "You can google

'Colburn family tragedy' and it'll pop up as a top hit." I inhale and exhale slowly. "He didn't realize his muscle relaxers would mix poorly with a drink or two, and he was impaired. He struck a bus."

Mrs. Barrett's face falls. "I'm so sorry."

"My mother and father, my grandmother, my siblings, their spouses, and my two nephews." My voice drops to a whisper. "And my husband. Also, another eight people on the bus. They all died."

Mrs. Barrett looks as sick as I feel.

"I was in the hospital for almost a week, but I recovered." My right hand goes to my left wrist compulsively. It may always feel a little messed up, but the doctors reassure me that with the screws and plate, it should function fine. "That was almost a year and a half ago, now."

"Mrs. Colburn, I'm sorry for pressing, but you see, as a social worker, I'm here to make sure this is a safe home for a child."

"And you think, based on what you've seen, that I'm unstable." In spite of my best efforts, my voice hikes up at the end, like a crazy person's.

"On the contrary," she says. "I've been looking for a support system. You seem to have no shortage of people who care for you."

My phone rings. The screen says Barbara. Corey must have called her.

"I assume that's a friend, calling because your other friend messed up."

I swallow and nod.

"You appear to have adjusted as well as anyone could to such a tragedy, and now you're making your ancestral home into an inn with the help of a competent and concerned partner. You're clearly surrounded by friends who care about you."

"Thank you."

"But most importantly. . . When someone decides to foster a child, there's always a reason." Mrs. Barrett grimaces. "Many times, the reasons aren't good. People want money. They want control over another human. Often, when the potential foster parent is not a relative and they request a particular child, they want to foster for all the wrong reasons."

"Wait." Now I feel really, really icked out. "What reason could I have for wanting to foster a particular child?"

Mrs. Barrett swallows. "You're only fourteen years older than him."

And I want to sink into the ground.

"I was tasked to find out whether there was anything inappropriate in the petition, but you appear to want to do it for all the right reasons. You're healing from your own tragedy, and you saw someone involved in a problem of their own. Now you want to help."

I stare at her. I know there are gross people out there, but thinking of how gross hurts me.

"Wanting to help someone else with their suffering after surviving yours, my dear Mrs. Colburn, is the best possible reason to want to foster a child."

"But my life's not full of good luck," I say. "I'm a little worried that in my efforts to help, I might just drag him down further." After making that confession, I feel a little better. Less guilty.

Mrs. Barrett smiles—beams might be a better description. "My dear girl." She sits on the edge of the blue corduroy sofa, and she pats the edge of the chaise lounge.

I sit.

"Salmon swim upstream. It's hard, but it gets them where they need to be to spawn. It takes all they have. Sunflowers grow toward the sunlight. They turn their big, heavy faces, all full of seeds, right at the sunshine. They wither and die before those seeds can sprout. Muscles in your body build from resistance. You only get stronger after you break them down."

"But—"

"You're talking about fostering a teenager. He's mostly baked already. You won't find the answers to what he needs from a book or a class, more than likely. But if you're ready to love him through all of it, if you're ready to take him as he is, then you may be just exactly what he needs." She lowers her voice. "And he may be what you need, too."

I start to cry then.

"You said you have bad luck, but girl, very few people in this world have luck as bad as the kids I see every single day in the foster system. As I walked through your house, you looked guilty and concerned. My job was to figure out why." She places a hand over mine. "You seem to think having a jug of bleach on the shelf of your laundry room would scare me. Some of the homes I evaluate have guns just lying on the coffee tables. There are often drugs hidden in the tanks of the bathroom toilets." Mrs. Barrett sighs. "All I was looking to uncover with you was a purpose."

I think about that day in the hardware store. "I was drowning," I say. "I survived the crash, and my body recovered, but I felt like I was slowly suffocating in my own life."

Mrs. Barrett just nods.

"Shortly before that day I met Emerson, I met

Dave. He felt like sunshine on my face. He suggested that instead of selling my grandmother's house, we could remodel it together and make it into an inn. That helped me a lot. I thought I would hate everything about the process, but I didn't."

"And?"

"Then we went to the hardware store to get some tools, some things to fix up some old furniture we found in the attic. And that's when I saw him. Emerson gave me some tips on plants, and he was the sweetest, kindest kid."

Tears are streaming down my face.

"I lost my baby that day, after the accident," I say. "I haven't told anyone that." Now I'm bawling like a lunatic. I can barely speak for the tears. "I was five months pregnant. The impact from the crash caused a uterine rupture, and with all the other trauma, they didn't even know what had happened." I can barely breathe, much less talk, but I have to force the words out. "They had to take out my uterus to stop the bleeding." I wipe my eyes.

Mrs. Barrett squeezes my hand. "I'm so very sorry."

"I can't have kids." My tears dry up for some reason. They just disappear. "That day, when Emerson told me he didn't have a mom. . ." I shrug. "I don't know why, exactly, except that I lost my child, and he lost his mother. My heart just looked at him, and it said, *yes*." I look at Mrs. Barrett. "Does that make me crazy?"

She shakes her head, and a tear rolls down her cheek, too. "No. I think you sound called, my dear. I think you've been sent to help this lost, lonely little boy."

We sit like that, just staring at one another for a moment. And then another. Neither of us speaks, but it heals something inside my soul. I just *know* that my home study is going to be a good one. Mrs. Barrett may have been skeptical at first, but not by the time she leaves. By then, she's Team Seren.

I can tell.

"May I give you just two suggestions?" she asks, as she's walking out the door.

"Of course," I say. "Please do."

"First, you have a man in your life who clearly cares a great deal about you. He may not be showing it in the best way, but don't be so quick to chase him away."

"Things are just complicated with Corey."

"Corey?" Mrs. Barrett's lip curls. "He's not very considerate, and you clearly don't trust him if he didn't even know about this." She shakes her head. "I meant Dave. That man stood here, making the most atrocious puns and stupid jokes I have ever heard, while his friend ran across the way to track you down. He looked more nervous than any dad I've seen waiting in a hospital for a newborn baby."

That shuts me up.

Dave.

She was talking about Dave.

"We're just partners, though," I say. "I wasn't making that up."

"All I'm saying is, you should give him a chance. There aren't many guys like that one."

I blink.

"And second. . .telling you this may be going too far. If it is, I'm sorry. But in my experience, the things we keep to ourselves are often the deepest wounds.

You want to deal with those as soon as you're able, or they'll come back to bite you."

My baby. She thinks I need to talk to someone about losing her.

"I tried therapy, but it was just—"

"I don't even mean therapy, necessarily. But maybe Dave. Or that woman who called you. Or just talking about babies when they come up." She shrugs. "You'll be the one who knows best how to handle it, but you can't keep the windows closed forever. Someday you'll have to let the light back in."

I think about her words all night.

And the next morning, too.

Dave still hasn't moved his stuff out. I'm sure Bentley's at work, and he can't move it by himself. Either way, it feels like I made a huge step forward, and now I'm treading water again.

I ought to ask him when he's leaving, and badger him for a plan and a timeline, but the woman's words keep coming back to me.

There aren't many guys like that one. Don't chase him away.

Whether he's a gem or not, he has no interest in me. And even if he did, I already told him we can never date. He'd have to sell me his shares in the company if we did. I couldn't even afford to buy them.

The second I finish placing my first order for toiletries, I collapse on the office chair. "I had no idea how annoying all the small things would be."

Dave laughs. "The story of my life."

"What do you mean?"

"You know my family owns landfills, right?"

I nod.

"My dad sort of passed most of the management of

the company off to me during my senior year in college. He had a 'minor heart event.'" He makes air quotes like it wasn't a big deal, but I can tell he was worried. "He wasn't supposed to be stressed. I thought it would be easy to handle the business since it had been run by a high school dropout for a long time, but there were so many small details. I had to apply for so many approvals, and pay for lots of licenses, and make sure I ordered and checked on a ridiculously long list of other items. From so many places." He laughs. "My dad sort of did things as they came up, but I wanted to get ahead of stuff. I thought we should be early for once."

"And?"

He collapses on the chair next to me. "It was harder than I thought."

"How'd you survive all that while you were a student, too?"

"I got really good with Excel." He laughs. "But also, I got very poor grades."

This time, I laugh.

"Aren't you happy to hear that about your partner?"

"I'm actually really happy you found me that day and suggested all this," I say. "It's been a lot to deal with some days, but you've been great." And it's good to have a reason to wake up every morning. None of my fears came true. "To be honest, I worried we'd fight about everything."

"So did I," he says. "I'm not always easy to get along with."

"Are you kidding?" I can barely believe it. "You agree with everything I suggest."

His cheeks turn red, for some reason.

"But look, Dave. I've been thinking about this."

Can I actually bring up the dating clause? Can I tell him I think it's stupid?

No.

No way. I can't do it.

His phone rings, which spares me. "Hello?"

I lean a bit closer, listening closely. I can usually recognize most of the people who call him now. This time, it's his sister, Danika.

"No, I'm still positive."

About what?

"Guys may regularly come to baby showers now, but *this guy* doesn't."

Oh. Her baby shower.

"I'm not kidding, D. It's not going to happen. Can you imagine what would—" He laughs. "Bring *a date*? To a baby shower? I can't think of a better way to freak out any girl I might like."

Another thing Mrs. Barrett said hits me then.

I should talk about babies.

Celebrate babies.

Just the thought has me breathing faster. But it's *both* the things she told me to do. All rolled up with a bow on top. It feels like a sign or something. And I never get signs.

"I'll go," I say. "I can be your date to the baby shower."

Dave turns toward me slowly, his expression incredulous. "You?"

I shrug. "Or not, if you don't want to."

"No." He shakes his head.

I hate how lousy it makes me feel. I mean, obviously he doesn't want to date me. I knew that. But is the idea of taking me *that* ridiculous?

"Are you sure you're willing to go with me?" he asks. "It's going to be really annoying."

The voice is tinny and small, but I hear Danika now that the phone's not so close to his ear. "It's not annoying! She'll love it."

That makes me smile. "Tell her I'm looking forward to it."

Danika squeals. "See you both tomorrow."

❧ 12 ❧

DAVE

anika learned what not to do by hearing about my experience at school. From day one, she told everyone that her parents ran a recycling center. It's technically true, of course. They offer recycling services in conjunction with the regular trash pickup. If I had thought of that, it might have been a smoother experience for me at school, too.

Although, I've never had Danika's intuitive sense for people. The woo is strong with her—she can figure out just what to say to make people like her, to distract them from any criticism, and to make sure she's the center of attention. She's the screaming neon extrovert to my introvert, and she makes sure everyone knows it.

Another key difference between my little sister and me is that, by the time she was in school, my parents had enough money for her to put herself front and center for parties, for events, and for school activities. She did dance team, with its huge price tag, and she hosted small parties at the house fairly often. We had a nice enough house by then that we fit in with the other posh kids with whom we went to school. It's probably the reason that, while I have two friends, Danika has dozens and dozens. So many I can't even keep them all straight.

It's also the reason I'm delighted to have Seren with me. I mean, other than the fact that she called herself my date, which sent a little thrill up my whole body, she'll keep me safe from Danika's never-ending machinations. It's been years since I've attended an event—any event—where she hasn't tried to set me up.

Unless I bring a date.

Although right now, my date looks practically ill. She's staring straight ahead, her hands clutched on the armrests in my car, a small pink gift resting on her lap. The color seems to have drained from her face, as if she's about to face a firing squad.

"You're really just going as my shield, you know," I say. "My sister tries to set me up with her friends every single time I'm anywhere in the vicinity."

"Would that be so bad?" she asks. "You like your sister. I imagine her friends are lovely."

I snort. "They're sent toward me like torpedoes."

"Torpedoes that want. . .what?" she asks. "To blow you up?" She arches one eyebrow.

"To marry me," I say.

She rolls her eyes. "Poor, poor Dave. His sister loves him and wants him to find a nice girl to marry. It must be so hard to be you."

This isn't going well at all. "It's not that."

"I know. I heard you before. Marriage is the end of everything." Her tone's flat, like she's super annoyed.

Could she be annoyed. . .because she likes me? I'm

probably just being a narcissist. "Not with the right person, maybe."

"Ho, ho, ho, that's a new tune." There's a little more color in her face, at least. Not enough to make me hope, but it's something.

"What is?"

"You think that, with the *right person*, that marriage might not be so bad?" Her half smile energizes me.

"Isn't that the point of every Disney movie? You just have to find that right person. The one who makes the thief into an honest hero. The one who changes the beast into a prince."

She rolls her eyes. "Please. All men are beasts. It's the prince that's the lie. Besides. That beast was hotter than the weird-looking cartoon guy they replaced him with. I think all the women in America will agree with me—bring back the beast."

"Well, listen, you're doing me a favor today, whether you meant to or not. So all you have to do if it gets to be too much is tell me that your vet called and you have to go."

"I don't have a vet," she says. "I don't even have a pet."

"That's the point," I say. "That's what makes it a code."

"But what if your sister hears? Then she'll want to know what pet I have."

Seren's the most ridiculous person in the world.

Is that why I adore her so much?

"Then let's say it's time to water your plants."

"Who has to water their plants at a certain time?" She shakes her head. "We can say it's time to give my friend Barbara a ride."

"Great," I say. "Let's go with that."

And then we're at my mom's house, which literally looks like it's vomiting pink. Rosy balloons are bunched around the stone mailbox, billowing from the front porch, and bundled into a huge archway over the door.

As we approach, I realize there's a pink carpet leading into the house, and bunches of petal-pink carnations are in pink vases on the front porch table, on the floor by the door, and on the entry hall table, which I can already see through the open door.

"Dave!" My mother lifts her arms and shouts. "You came."

"I did."

She jogs toward me, like always, her substantial body practically jiggling with her joy to see me. Her lipstick and blush are both bright pink, and as she envelops me in one of her mama-bear hugs, I look around and realize it's not only her.

It appears everyone else got the memo as well. All around us, everyone's wearing pink. Pale pink dresses. Hot pink pants. Pink floral blouses, pink striped pants, pink, pink, pink.

"No one told me I had to wear a pink polo shirt."

"Or me," Seren says. "I'm sorry I'm out of dress code." She looks amazing in her bright yellow sundress and little strappy sandals. I hate that she feels uncomfortable.

"You threw the invite away, didn't you?" Mom asks.

I scratch my head. "Well, it's not so much that I threw it away as that I never saw it."

"You don't check your mail?" Mom tsks. "How do you expect to run a business when—"

"I pay everything online, Mom. My mail's just spam and catalogs."

"But you still need to—"

"I haven't been living at home," I say in exasperation. "I've been staying at the inn, because we launch in a few weeks. I'm over there all the time."

Mom blinks. "Isn't that woman there, too? So are you living together?"

"Mom." I wrap an arm around Seren's shoulders. "This is *that* woman. Try to be a little bit polite, or people will think your mom never taught you manners."

Mom's eyes bulge. "She's—you're—" Mom swallows. "I'm so sorry. It's wonderful to meet you." She holds out her hand, her fingernails polished bright pink. "Dave is just awful, never updating me on anything."

Seren smiles shyly. "It's so nice to meet you, Mrs. Fansee. You've raised a wonderful son."

"He has nothing but glowing reports about you, and we're all very excited for the inn to open."

"Thanks," Seren says. "It's been a strange few weeks, changing the old house into a place people can stay over, but it's been exciting, too."

"Change isn't ever easy," Mom says. "You're brave for embracing it. Dave tells us that the stupid government stole half the value of the house in taxes." Mom shakes her head. "It's criminal, really."

Luckily, Mom doesn't bring up the accident. Every time it comes up with new people, Seren cringes. I'd really rather avoid that.

Especially on, well, kind of on our first date.

"Let's go grab something to eat," I say. "You've met my mom, and any time now Danika will descend."

"Okay," Seren says.

But it's too late. Something alerted my sister,

maybe hearing her own name, and she's coming for us. "Dave!"

My mother's loud, but she's nothing to Danika. Police sirens are nothing to Danika. It'll be a wonder if her baby isn't born with hearing loss. As she walks toward us—lumbers is a better word—I think about how interesting it is to watch your mother in a younger, smaller form. She shakes just like Mom, but with excitement, not from fat jiggles. She's louder, and more animated, and just *extra* everything.

"You came, and you brought a date, and *look* at her. Seren, you're just stunning!" She's picking up speed now, and I actually worry she might not be able to stop. What happens if a pregnant woman plows into a crowd of people? Maybe she'll hit Mom and bounce backward.

Or would that be worse?

This time, I open my arms for a hug, hoping to protect Seren and help Danika stop at the same time. "So excited to meet this little girl."

Danika, to my surprise, doesn't plow into me. She manages to stop herself—no collision at all. That's a relief. "Are you? You never came by after Todd was born."

"I came over and stayed for three nights when your husband was out of town, and I came by every single Sunday for the first year of his life."

She rolls her eyes. "Other than that."

I can't help laughing. She's *so* dramatic. "I'll try and do better with this one."

"Todd talks about you all the time. He calls you his handsome uncle."

"Well, it's me or Oliver." I can't help making a face.

"That's not very nice," Seren says.

163

"Oliver's my in-law's dog," Danika says. "They don't have another son." She laughs. "And Dave, you did not tell me your business partner looks *just like* her famous grandmother. Holy cow, you could be on all the billboards for the inn." She shakes her head. "No, you *should* be on all the billboards. You're the spitting image of Audrey Colburn."

"I do hear that a lot," Seren says.

"But unlike you, Seren doesn't *like* being the center of attention," I say. "So when I suggested it, she didn't want to be on the billboards, the fliers, or any of the other marketing stuff."

Danika shakes her head. "The most beautiful faces always go to the wrong people." She leans closer, her eyes intent. "I would switch with you in a heartbeat." My sister bites her lip. "How did my brother ever find a girl like you?"

"Well," Seren says. "When he met me, I might have looked a bit like the inn looked at first."

"The inn?" Danika asks.

"It was a fixer upper," Seren says. "And so was I. Let's just say that."

"No way," Danika says. "He called me that day, and while he didn't say you were gorgeous, he was already giddy about the house."

"That's kind of him," Seren says. "He's someone who manages to see the potential in things."

"He always has," Danika says.

"Remember that time he brought home that old junker car?" Mom asks. "We all thought he'd lost his mind. But after he redid the paint and replaced the upholstery—"

"And fixed most everything else," Danika says.

"He sold it for a fortune." Mom looks smug.

"I hope he doesn't sell me," Seren says.

Mom and Danika both laugh.

"I'd kill him if he ever tried," Mom says.

"Hey, how did Dad get out of coming to this?" I ask.

"Oh, he didn't," Mom says. "He's just hiding in the kitchen with a few of the other men."

"Why did they decide the guys have to come to these now?" I ask.

"It's enlightened," Danika says. "You didn't hear?"

"Plus, she gets more gifts this way," Mom says.

"I really need a new diaper genie," Danika says. "Todd destroyed the last one."

"Could I have sent a bigger check and gotten out of it?" I ask.

"Not a chance," Danika says. "I wanted to meet this one." She takes Seren's arm and starts trundling her off.

Oh, no, no, no. I follow.

"Let them go." Mom grabs my arm. "Give your sister a minute with her."

"That's what I'm afraid to do," I say. "We aren't dating, Mom. This is our first event out together. Ever."

Mom lifts her eyebrows. "Even better."

"You guys are kind of a lot," I say. "I really don't want you to scare her off."

"I knew you liked her."

"How could I not?" It feels strange to admit it out loud.

Mom squeals, of course. "Oh, I thought this would never happen. Do you know how badly I want some of your grandbabies?"

I practically smash my hand over her mouth. "For the love of—Mom. Stop. Now."

She rolls her eyes. "Fine. Fine. But I'm entitled to be excited."

"Just go slow with this one. She startles easy."

"That's why our family's great. We're like steam-rollers." Mom smiles. "We'll flatten out any objections she may have."

That's exactly what I'm afraid of. "Please, no steam-rolling. Promise me."

"If she's good enough for my son, then she's—"

"Mom, we can talk about it later, okay? But for now, just act like we're friends, and don't be pushy. Basically, don't be you." I eye her. "I mean it."

Mom huffs, but I can tell she heard me. I should be safe. Or more importantly, Seren should be safe.

It takes me fifteen minutes or so to work my way through the various cousins, old family friends, and aunts to where Danika's holding court with Seren by her side. But finally, I get there.

And miracle of miracles, my gorgeous partner doesn't even look too horrified or shell-shocked.

"Yes, this is Seren. She's Dave's girlfriend. Isn't she stunning? It figures that the prettiest person in our family would end up with a girlfriend who looks like a movie star." Danika's beaming.

My sister looks beautiful, actually. Even heavier than she's ever been. Even tired and a little worn thin. For maybe the first time, I see what people mean when they say pregnant people are glowing, because she's clearly very happy. It shows.

That makes me wonder how she'll look with a black eye, because I'm about to punch her. If she says Seren's my girlfriend *one more time*...

166

Except. . .Seren's rolling with it.

She didn't object.

She didn't freak out.

She didn't even look dismayed.

Is it possible that she's fine with being introduced as my girlfriend? And if so. . .*why?*

Does she like me? My heart starts to race. Or does she just figure it's the way things happen at family events? Is she just putting on a good face until she can get out of here? I don't know her well enough yet to know what her serene, impassive expression means. Is she really calm, or is she shoving her panic or irritation deep, deep down?

"—believe that he's finally got a girlfriend." Danika's stupid sorority sister Hayley is staring at Seren like she's a bug. "What did you do, exactly, to land him?"

"She did nothing," I say. "I fell for her precisely because she didn't try to *land me.*"

The head of every single woman in the room whips toward me, and I know how a gazelle that stumbles upon a pride of lions feels. I blink. "Oh, I'm sorry. I was told that men were invited to this shower, but clearly this is a Y-chromosome-free zone." I hold out my hand. "Isn't it about time for us to go pick up Barbara?"

"Wait." Danika's face ping pongs between me and Seren. "Who's Barbara?"

"She's Seren's best friend. Her car's in the shop, and we have to pick her up from the yoga studio."

"There aren't many Barbaras out there," Danika says. "Especially ones who work at yoga places. Could she possibly be the one who runs Namas-Day?"

Seren blinks. "Do you know her?"

Danika squeals again, and I swear, it's a miracle

none of the glass shatters. I've never appreciated Seren's understated calm more than I do in this moment. "You know her too? I just love her. We used to go clubbing sometimes."

"Wait," Seren says. "Are you. . . *Danny*?"

This time, I can feel Danika's squeal before it happens, like she's sucking all the air in the room up in anticipation of it.

Seren actually smiles, even in the middle of it, when we're all doing our best not to cover our ears and duck under the coffee table.

"I didn't know she had a car. I thought she took the subway."

"It was your brother's secret code," Seren says. "To get us out of here." She smiles at me. "But I'm fine. We don't need to leave."

Danika roars with laughter and pats her leg. "I just love you. I may steal you from my fumbly brother if he's not careful." Danika leans closer. "It *is* the twenty-twenties, you know."

Mom rolls her eyes. When Danika's too ridiculous even for her, I know it's gone too far. Before I can intervene, Mom says, "I think it's time to open presents."

"I want to open Seren's first," Danika says.

I cringe a little. I have no idea what she brought, and I don't want to put her on the spot. "How about you open *mine* first?" I ask. "It's much bigger, and I know you want it."

"You're such an attention hog," Danika says. "But today I'm way more excited about Seren than I am about you." She points at the massive pile of gifts on the table next to Seren. "Which one is yours?"

"This one." Seren picks up the small, flat, pink-wrapped box from the bottom at the front, somehow managing not to dislodge any of the fourteen gift bags on top of and beside it, and hands it to Danika.

I can barely breathe while I wait for Danika to open it. One of her most pronounced shortcomings is that she's categorically unable to pretend to like something if she doesn't. If this is a blinged pacifier or a designer burp cloth, we're all set. But if Seren went for one of her typical, understated items, or some kind of special cooking gadget, we may be in for an awkward interchange. My sister's more of a put-the-best-take-out-on-speed-dial gal.

My mom looks as nervous as I am, all her attention on Danika's hands as she unwraps the gift.

"It looks like a tie," one of Seren's friends says.

"It's not long enough for that," another says. "And why would she get a tie for a baby girl?"

"Burp rags?" someone else guesses.

But Danika opens it then, with the lid facing out. No one else can see what it is, but her face tells me it's not a burp rag. Danika—my flamboyant, always-on sister—freezes. And then tears well up in her eyes.

When I glance sideways at Seren, she has tears in her eyes, too.

What on earth did she give her?

Mom's seemingly speechless, which is probably a first. I can't think of another single time my mom had nothing to say.

At any event, ever.

"What is it?" Hayley asks. "We're all waiting."

Danika swallows, lifts something out of the box, and turns it around. I have to squint. It's a. . .needlepoint?

It's probably the most delicate, most beautiful

needlepoint I've ever seen. The words, *Mom loves you forever, little one*, stand out in a soft, pale blue. But the rest of the framed display is full of tiny flowers, butterflies, and greenery.

"Did you do that yourself?" Mom asks.

"Of course she did," Danika says.

"How do you know?" Hayley asks.

"I can tell," my sister says, softly.

"I did make it," Seren says.

I'm left wondering *how* she could possibly have made that between last night and this morning. Did she stay up all night? Is she secretly a needlepoint wizard? Does that even exist?

"Who taught you?" Mom asks.

"My grandmother," Seren says. "She actually started this one for me." She points. "She did that butterfly."

Murmurs start up around the room. "Her grandmother—"

"Heard she's famous."

"Audrey Colburn."

"Looks just like her."

"I heard she died."

"Are you sure you don't want to keep this?" Danika asks, her voice as soft as I've ever heard from her at a public gathering. "I love it, but I'd hate for you to regret giving it to me."

Seren shakes her head, but her smile concerns me.

It's dead-eyed.

Something's wrong.

Danika moves along, opening my deluxe diaper genie, piles of baby blankets, designer clothing and burp rags, stuffed animals, swaddling blankets, and a million other things.

Through all of that, Seren's smile never changes.

"I can't wait," Mom says, luckily in a low voice, "for the baby shower we'll throw for you one day. If you marry Seren, can you imagine the beauty of those babies?" She shivers. "I just adore her already."

Something Mom says helps pieces in my brain to click into place.

Seren had that needlepoint already.

She was married.

She lost *everyone*.

Is it that much of a stretch? It wasn't in any of the reports or articles, but could she have lost a child? Was that needlepoint. . .for her baby? Surely not.

I pull my phone from my pocket. "Oh, no."

Seren looks up at me.

"We've got a small emergency at the inn," I say. "We need to meet the plumber out there immediately."

Seren shoots to her feet and follows me out carefully, avoiding meeting anyone else's eye.

"You didn't have to bring a present," I say.

"I wanted to."

I don't press further until we reach the car. She's buckling when I come clean. "There's nothing wrong at the inn. But something is wrong with you. I could tell."

She freezes, looking down at her hands, which are now frozen on the buckle.

"If you want to talk about it, great. If not, that's fine too. I'm taking you home either way. But if you change your mind, I can get that needlepoint back, no questions asked."

She shakes her head slowly.

"That's fine, too. Danika loves it."

She nods.

The entire drive back, she simply stares out the window. I park in the garage spot next to her car, and prepare myself that she may leave the car just like she's been for the whole drive. No words. No explanation. Nothing.

But then she turns.

"I was pregnant with a little girl when my dad crashed the rental van." She's looking down at her lap, but I see tears falling on her skirt. "She didn't make it." A sob wracks her tiny frame.

I don't know what to do.

Do I put a hand on hers? Do I stay sitting here, like a giant, useless lump?

"And then—they had to do a surgery. To stop the bleeding." Now she starts to bawl in earnest, great, heaving sobs. "They took my uterus out." She wipes at her eyes. "I can't ever have kids."

When she looks up at me, she's not dead-eyed. The pain is raw and real.

But she still looks dead inside.

"Oh, Seren." I reach across the gear shift and drag her toward my chest. It's the most awkward position I've ever been in with a girl, and my heart is breaking, and I don't know how to make any of it better. "I'm sorry."

"I can't do this." She shoves back against the door of the car. "I said we can't date? Remember?"

I'm having trouble keeping up.

"That's why. I can't have kids. You could never have kids with me. Never." She opens the door and shoots out, like a trespasser fleeing the police.

Should I follow her?

Or do I stay?

I wish life came with a guidebook. When I used to have time to play video games, I loved this one called Final Fantasy. If you really got stuck, you could go online or pay gurus for advice. They'd tell you how to beat the masters, how to find secret caches of objects. How to find backdoors. None of that exists in real life. No, I'm stuck flailing around like the big, clumsy idiot that I am.

I've never cared as much about my failure to understand what to do or say in any situation as I do right now.

I think about what I know about Seren, what I've seen, heard, and witnessed her doing in the last two months. She's straightforward, focused on the now, and pragmatic. She's not a pie-in-the-sky lady. I wonder if she was always this way, or if she's been forced to start taking things one day at a time. Either way, it's the Seren I know. She looks at the current issues and deals with them. She only looks at the future when pressed.

Except for that day in the hardware store. She went to check out plants for the house, and she came back with outdoor plants instead.

And a juvenile delinquent she wanted to foster.

I've always admired her desire to help Emerson, but I didn't really understand it until right now. She lost her parents, her siblings, their kids, her grandmother, her husband, everyone.

And her baby.

Emerson lost his mother, but I gather she was all he had.

It's so obvious, I hate that I never thought of it before.

Seren has a heart as big as the ocean, and she

thinks she's bad luck for everyone she meets. She told me that on the first day. Meanwhile, she's done nothing but bring joy and light into my life.

While dealing with all this on her own.

She thought that she and her husband would welcome a child into a loving home. Instead, she came home with empty arms and a broken heart.

It feels like my heart's breaking inside my chest.

I'm not someone who takes on the pain of others very often. I let them deal with their issues, and I focus on mine. But I wish, in this moment, that I could take Seren's. I wish there was anything at all I could do to ease the pain in her heart.

And then I have an idea.

I practically race from the car toward the carriage house. I don't bother knocking, because I still haven't moved out.

And now, hopefully I won't.

Seren's curled up on the blue corduroy sofa, sobbing.

"Are you alright?" I ask, tentatively.

She sits up slowly, wiping her tears on the arm of the sofa. "You know, the hardest thing about life isn't living."

"No?" I sit down next to her carefully.

"It's the unmet expectations. If I hadn't been so excited for that baby, if I hadn't been so set on being a mother." She draws in a ragged breath. "It might not have wrecked me as much. I might have recovered better."

"You're doing really well," I say. "I'm proud of you."

"Here's the thing," she says. "I try really hard not to get caught up in the despair that always follows thinking about what I wanted and what I'll never have."

That's why she's so desperate to help Emerson. "I want to foster Emerson, too. With you."

"You what?"

"I said, I want to foster him with you. I don't want to move out. You shouldn't have to do this alone."

"I don't need help," she says. "I can do it alone."

I sit down next to her and take her hand in mine. "I know you *can*, but that doesn't mean you should."

"But we aren't even dating."

"About that." A wave of fear wells up inside of me, telling me to keep my mouth shut.

I push past it.

"I like you. I've liked you since that very first day. When you popped up in bed, like a late-spring daisy, with that Cheerio on your cheek." I chuckle. "I still see it whenever I think of that memory. You were glorious."

She bats at my hand. "That's not funny."

"You were." I take her hand again. This time, I hold on with purpose. "I want to date you. And if that means you want to buy my shares, well. I'm not too worried."

"You aren't?"

I lean closer, my eyes intent on hers. "You're flat broke, you know."

"I am not." She lifts her nose. "I have an inn."

"You have *half* an inn," I clarify. "And I own the other half."

She frowns.

"And I'd like to propose that you work with me on another project, since this one's going so well."

"Emerson isn't a project," she says. "He's a long-term commitment. I don't know what he may do or say, but it could be bad. For a long time. A lot of foster kids test you. They don't feel lovable, so they act unlovable to see if you'll cut them loose."

I shrug. "Okay."

"It's going to be hard, and I know that. I can't have someone else who isn't totally committed."

"I agree. But I am totally committed. Let me help —and let me take you out. It's a package deal, in my mind."

"Emerson and I aren't a buy-one-get-one." She's half-smiling, so I think that's progress.

"What if I don't want to date you either?"

She blinks. "I thought you just said—"

"Don't date me," I say. "Just be my girlfriend. My committed, live-in girlfriend."

Her eyes widen and her breaths become shallow. "I —that's—we haven't even—"

"I know. You haven't even kissed me, right?" I step toward her, and her head turns upward, her eyes meeting mine. My voice drops, and now I'm talking to her low and slow. "You might hate me. I might not like you."

She just told me about her baby. She ran into her house and started bawling. I can't imagine a time that's less hot than that.

But being with Seren isn't about things being *hot*. That may have been what my past relationships were about. Attraction. Sparks. And that's important, but it's not enough, alone.

For the first time ever, just being with a woman is already enough, because Seren's got heart like no one I've ever met.

She's staggeringly beautiful.

She's reliable, too.

And talented in so many ways that I keep discovering more.

But most of all, she has hope when anyone else—when *everyone* else—I know would've given up.

That gives me hope, too, that when it comes down to it, when it really matters, she'll be there for me. She'll be okay with my flaws, with my inadequacies, and she'll love me like I love her.

It slams into me like a Mack truck in that moment.

I love Seren Colburn.

I love her wit. Her generosity. Her sense of purpose. I love her fierce desire to protect and her work ethic. I love her snark and her kindness. And most of all, I love the way she stares misery in the face, the way she faces off against her awful bad luck, and she gives it the bird.

She's fierce.

The kindest, most gentle warrior I've ever met.

So I wrap my arms around my little warrior, and I pull her against my chest. I lower my head slowly, giving her every chance she might need to turn away. To deny the garbage guy that I am, deep down in my heart of hearts.

But she doesn't.

She looks up at me with shining eyes.

I press my lips to hers.

And she whimpers. My arms tighten. My mouth presses closer. Hers meets mine hungrily, and her small arms circle my waist. "I think," I whisper against her mouth, "that we'll fit just fine."

✣ 13 ✣

SEREN

I have a memorable name.

In all my life, I've never met anyone else named Serendipity.

Certainly not Serendipity Colburn.

It's not like my name is one that's easy to mistake for someone else's. And like it or not, my face is pretty recognizable, too. But once, when I was fifteen, I was at a National Honor Society meeting, and this woman thought I was her son's girlfriend. She gushed. She complimented. She acted like I was the most amazing girl in the world. For a brief moment in time, I felt really, really special.

Of course, when her son showed up, he cleared things up, and then the woman looked at me like I was a mental case. "Why didn't you say it wasn't you?"

That's how I thought things would go when Dave found me at the shower. Surely he'd tell his sister and her friends that I had not in fact 'landed' the hottest guy I'd met.

He wasn't my boyfriend.

Only, this time, the guy didn't out me. He just

178

smiled. He leaned against the wall in the corner of the room, smiled at all those women, and played along. For the first time in my life, I almost understood my grandmother's occupation. It may not have been real, but it felt really amazing to sit there, next to the world's nicest mother-to-be, who was actually already a mother, and celebrate as though I was her, well, maybe someday her sister-in-law. I pretended that I was the one David Fansee chose, when he could have dated any girl in the room.

Of course, it wasn't real. I knew it wasn't real. And then, when he was so kind, so considerate, and so insightful that he realized I needed to get out of there, and then when he took me home. . . It only made it hurt more, knowing that we're *not* dating.

But then he said the words. The words that keep rattling around in my head like a dangerous viper.

"There's nothing wrong at the inn. But something is wrong with you. I could tell."

He's being all considerate and caring and just. . .it's too much.

I'm barely back on my feet.

I still wake up with Cheerios stuck to my face more often than not.

But I'm getting out of bed, and Emerson needs me to keep getting better. Otherwise, how can I help him? And as miserable as the last year has been, I was an adult when everything fell apart. Emerson's just a kid. So I run inside, hoping he'll let all of it go. Hoping he won't make me feel like a pathetic idiot for wanting to date him. I'm not sure I can take that.

But the doggedly persistent idiot follows me.

Again.

"Here's the thing," I say. "I try really hard not to

get caught up in the despair that always follows thinking about what I wanted and what I'll never have."

But he doesn't seem to get the message. His face is still all optimistic and chipper, like he's going to fix this, fix me. "I want to foster Emerson, too. With you."

"You what?"

"I said, I want to foster him with you. I don't want to move out. You shouldn't have to do this alone."

"I don't need help." There's no way Dave's as committed as I am. I wish that was my main reason for saying no, because for Emerson's sake, it should be. But it's more than that. I can't be part of a team again, only to lose it. It's better if I never have help to begin with. "I can do it alone." I *will* do it alone.

He still won't let it go. He sits down next to me, inching closer slowly, like I'm a wild animal in a nature preserve. He takes my hand in his. "I know you *can*, but that doesn't mean you should."

His hand is strong. Warm. Comforting.

Dangerous.

"But we aren't even dating."

"About that." His face—his gorgeous, makes-all-the-girls-stare-at-him-with-longing face is conflicted. What's he conflicted about? Me? "I like you. I have liked you since that very first day. When you popped up in bed, like a late-spring daisy, with that Cheerio on your cheek." He laughs a charming, I'm-almost-embarrassed-at-how-handsomely-precious-I-am laugh. "I still see it whenever I think of that memory. You were glorious."

I knock his hand away. "That's not funny."

"You were." He reaches for me again, and I can't

180

resist him. He's too persistent. Too insistent. And then he says the words my heart has been yearning to hear without me even knowing it. "I want to date you. And if that means you want to buy my shares, well. I'm not too worried."

Because he wants out? "You aren't?"

His cocky half-smile is overkill. "You're flat broke, you know."

"I am not." I lift my chin. "I have an inn."

"You have *half* an inn, and I own the other half."

That's a rude thing to point out. But he's also right. I can't really buy him out when my major asset is the other half of what he owns.

"And I'd like to propose that you work with me on another project, since this one's going so well."

"Emerson isn't a project." The fact that he'd say that just shows that it's a lark for him. "He's a long-term commitment. I don't know what he may do or say, but it could be bad. For a long time. A lot of foster kids test you. They don't feel lovable, so they act unlovable to see if you'll cut them loose."

He doesn't waver. "Okay."

Even when I throw out a bunch of objections and explain how hard it will be, he's still insistent. So I press again.

"It's going to be hard," I say, "and I know that. I can't have someone else who isn't totally committed."

"I agree, but I am totally committed. Let me help —and let me take you out. It's a package deal, in my mind."

"Emerson and I aren't a buy-one-get-one." Is he kidding?

"What if I don't want to date either?"

Was it all a joke? Was he messing with me? "I thought you just said—"

"Don't date me," he says. "Just be my girlfriend. My committed, live-in girlfriend."

Live-in? As in, he'd move into my room? My heart starts hammering in my chest, and I can barely breathe. "I—that's—we haven't even—"

"I know. You haven't even kissed me, right?" His self-confident grin tells me he's not worried about that part. "You might hate me. I might not like you." His voice is like warm butter, melting over hot toast.

And I think I'm the toast.

I've just been telling him how broken I am.

I can't have children.

Each morning is a battle. I always want to duck under the covers and never come out, but he's still looking at me like I hung the moon. He bites his full lip and shifts closer.

I can't help my tiny whimper.

His arms tighten around me as if he *liked* that. And then his lips come down to meet mine.

I thought if this moment ever came again, that I would be scared. That I might feel like I was betraying my husband, but I don't. All I feel is warm, and happy, and treasured.

Because Dave is safe.

Dave is my center.

And when my heart surges in my chest, when his arms pull me even closer, when his lips move against mine, everything feels hot and cold and up and down and right and wrong all at once.

Which is exactly how a kiss *should* feel.

I'd almost forgotten how it felt to be *alive* like this.

"I think," Dave says softly, "that we'll fit just fine."

It's quite a few moments before another thought finds room in my head. And by then, I'm sitting on Dave's lap, nestled against the corner of the blue corduroy sofa. When my phone rings, I scramble off his lap as though we've been caught.

Dave's grin has me blushing.

My caller ID tells me that it's the social worker from yesterday, Mrs. Barrett.

"Hello?"

"Mrs. Colburn?"

I clear my throat. "Yes, that's me."

"I just had a few questions I didn't get answered yesterday, and I thought I could check them with you over the phone."

"Actually," I say. "I. . .how big of a deal would it be for us to modify the home study?"

"Modify?"

"I finally told Seren how I feel about her," Dave's voice rumbles from over my shoulder. "I told her I don't want to move out."

"Oh." Mrs. Barrett's silent for a moment. "Well, can I just say, *not* as a social worker, *good for you*! But as a social worker. . .since I did meet you yesterday, maybe I can conduct a phone interview to get all of your information and simply modify the write-up a bit?"

"Sure," Dave covers my hand with his and lifts the phone out of my hand. "I'm all yours."

"You'll, of course, have to expedite your criminal background check and immediately complete the foster training. My understanding is we have just under three weeks until the subject—"

"Emerson Duplessis," Dave says.

"Right. Emerson will be out of juvenile hall."

"Yes."

The next hour's spent with Dave and I answering questions on the phone. We wind up putting it on speaker phone, so it's easier. And at the end, Mrs. Barrett doesn't even seem annoyed.

"Sorry for the change up," I say.

"Don't be sorry," Mrs. Barrett says. "I could tell he loved you, and I'm glad he finally told you himself."

When she hangs up, the word floats between us.

Love.

Luckily, Dave's stomach growls.

We both laugh.

"We should get a proper meal," Dave says. "We skipped out of the shower without getting much to eat, and then that woman talked our ears off."

"I can just make sandwiches," I say. "Or—"

Dave takes my hand. "I've been dreaming of taking you out for weeks and weeks. If all goes well, we'll have a kid, soon. Let me take you on a proper date while I can."

My heart does a cartwheel, and then I nod. "Okay."

Metro Deli's pretty nice for a deli—and we make it in time to order the Challah French toast, which makes me happy. Of course, Dave orders the Reuben, which cracks me up.

"You eat enough meat to make up for me being vegetarian." I cringe a little, looking at it.

"Does it bother you?" He drops his sandwich. "I'm sorry."

I shrug. "I'm mostly kidding—you're eating what you would have eaten whether I went without or not. I'm sure it's not a karmic wash."

"I could cut back," he says. "Maybe I should."

"Don't do it for me," I say. "But if you watched some videos of—"

He holds up his sandwich and shakes his head. "Not in the middle of a meal."

I shrug. "Fair enough."

"So, do you want to change everything about me?" He arches one eyebrow. "Sometimes my mom acts like that with my dad."

"So far, only the flesh eating," I say. "The rest I like."

"Really?" He grins. "Tell me more about what you like."

I roll my eyes. "I need to amend my prior statement. Other than the flesh-eating *and* the cockiness, I like the rest."

"Liar," he says. "Girls like confident guys."

"Eat your sandwich," I say. "That poor turkey already died. May as well make his sacrifice worth something."

He frowns. "Now that I'm thinking of a turkey dying, I kind of don't want this anymore."

I can't help laughing. "You'll get there eventually."

"Did you terrorize your family like this?" He's smiling, and then he freezes.

"Don't," I say.

"I'm sorry," Dave says. "I wasn't thinking."

I put a hand on his arm. "I didn't mean that you shouldn't mention them. I meant, don't freeze up when you do." I inhale sharply. "It still hurts to talk about them, but it's the good kind of hurt, like when your legs are sore, but you know walking will help ease it."

He nods.

"I didn't torment them," I say. "I guess I felt bad about it."

Dave smiles. "I'm glad."

"You're glad I didn't torment them?" I narrow my eyes. "Why?"

"Because." He leans closer. "If you never hassled them, but you do hassle me, that means I'm special."

I snort.

"I'm serious about this," Dave says. "I'm sure your first husband was lovely, but I mean to blow him out of the water."

That makes me laugh even harder, for some reason.

"I'm competing with a dead man," he says. "I'm not sure if that means I'm doomed to lose, or whether it gives me a fighting change."

Now I'm belly-laughing. People are staring. Normally, it would've made me uncomfortable. But for some reason, with Dave, I don't care.

Let them stare.

"Excuse me," the waitress says.

I immediately sober. This is why I'm usually more careful not to draw attention to myself. I hate causing scenes. "I'm so sorry," I say. "We'll be quiet."

"Oh, no." The waitress gulps. "That's not. . . I was wondering if you two are famous?"

"Excuse me?" Dave asks.

"You're both so beautiful," the waitress says. "And the customers at that table were asking, and we all thought we'd seen you on Instagram, or maybe on TikTok?" She's clutching a napkin.

As if we might sign it for her.

Now I'm really laughing. "Not famous," I say. "Just famously annoying. Sorry."

Dave shrugs. "Although, you are looking at Audrey

Colburn's granddaughter."

The waitress's jaw drops. "I knew it. I loved her so much in *Good Luck Bride*." She thrusts the napkin out. "Can you sign this? I'd love to pin it to my movie poster."

"But it wasn't me in the movie," I say.

"It was your grandmother," the waitress says. "And she looked just like you. Please?"

I snatch the napkin and scrawl my name on it.

"Wait, is your name Serendipity?" she asks. "That's amazing."

"We're actually opening an inn around the corner soon," Dave says. "It's in the very house her grandmother lived in her entire life. It's been refurbished, but we've kept most of it substantially the same."

The waitress's face lights up. "Get out."

"You should come check it out," Dave says. "The grand opening's in two weeks." He pulls a card out of his pocket.

"The Audrey Colburn Inn?" She shivers. "I love it."

"Wait, are you Audrey Colburn's granddaughter?" The lady from the table the waitress pointed at is standing by us now. "I'm her biggest fan."

This is getting more awkward by the moment.

"Klara," the man behind her says, "stop. They're eating."

"I just can't believe it." She's holding a napkin, too. "My goofy boyfriend *insisted* we come here, and I didn't want to. Can you imagine? What good luck that I listened to him." She crouches lower. "I owed him. He gave me the best back massage last night. But I just can't believe it worked out for me, too."

"Serendipity Inn," Dave says. "That's what we're renaming it."

I gasp. "What?"

"Anyone who comes to our inn gets good luck," Dave says. "Guaranteed."

I cannot believe what he's saying. "Hush."

The woman's clapping. "I'm an Instagram influencer," she says. "I have an apartment around the corner, but I'd love to be one of the first guests. Can I?" She swipes through her phone. "I usually do, like, makeup and beauty products, but this is still right on point for my brand, I swear."

"We're on a pretty tight budget," I say. "And—"

"Oh, I'll pay for the room." She smiles. "I just want to be there on the first night." Her face lights up. "Is there a spa?"

"Uh, not yet," I say. "But maybe soon."

She claps. "If you want tips or ideas, I'm your girl." She swivels her phone around. "Look. This is me."

SheShootsSheScores.

Really?

Then my eyes track downward to the followers.

Two million.

I swallow. "Um, sure. We can make sure you have a room the first night. Thanks."

"Here. Give me your handle, and I'll reach out."

My handle?

"I'll give you mine," Dave says. "She gets mobbed when she gets on social, as you can imagine."

"Totes," Klara says.

Totes? What is she saying?

A few moments later, Dave's making a note on the top of our receipt.

"What are you doing?"

His face turns red. "Should I not expense the meal from our first date?"

"You're. . .what?"

"But you and I came up with a way better name for the inn, the Serendipity, and also a tagline that plays into one of your grandmother's most famous and lasting films."

Good Luck Bride? Really?

"But I'm bad luck," I hiss. "Or did you forget?"

He shrugs. "Or think of it this way. If we all have a certain amount of bad and good luck in our lives, you've used up all your bad. That means it's nothing but good from here."

"I really don't think that's how it works," I say.

"How do you know?"

"Helen Keller."

"What?"

"Blind and deaf," I say. "Super unlucky."

"Oh." He nods. "Famous author, IQ off the charts, changed the world in many ways that helped people all over. Hit me again."

"Oh for the love," I say. "Princess Diana."

"You know, you're not helping your case," he says. "She may have ended her life unlucky, but for years and years, everyone in the world thought she was the luckiest woman alive. Chosen out of a million eligible applicants to become a princess. Two beautiful boys. What else you got?"

I roll my eyes.

"Look, all I'm saying is that now you have me. And I'm going to make sure that your luck's great from here on out."

"That's not how luck works," I say.

"And how would the world's unluckiest person know that?" He arches one eyebrow, and part of me really wants to believe him.

❧ 14 ❧

SEREN

I almost forgot I had plans with Barbara.

Actually, that's a lie.

I did forget.

I'm a lousy friend. Barbara shows up at my house with takeout from my favorite Chinese place—extra broccoli and snap peas, with fried tofu—and I'm sitting on the sofa with Dave, arguing about the changes to the name and logo for the inn.

"Do you want me to go?" Barbara asks.

Dave hops to his feet. "Not at all. I'll go join Bentley or Bernie with whatever they're doing. You two have fun."

Just like that, my shiny new boyfriend is gone, but Barbara has enough questions for two people.

"So you're dating."

"How do you know that?"

"You had your feet on his *lap* when I came in."

"No one knocks anymore," I grumble.

Barbara laughs.

I sit up, pulling my legs up against my chest in the corner of the sofa. "Are you mad?"

"Two months ago, you set me up with a guy who looks like Henry freaking Cavill. Then after almost two months, you're finally dating him, and you think I'm *mad*?"

"Yes?"

"Clearly he already liked you when you tried to set us up."

I blink, trying to follow her. "So you're not mad?"

She drops onto the other side of my sofa with a whoosh. "Not at all. I've been waiting for this eagerly." She leans closer. "In fact, it makes me feel better. If he'd completely rejected me for no reason, I'd feel like a loser. But if he was already smitten with my bestie but couldn't admit it, then of *course* he couldn't fall for me."

"I doubt he was already—"

"He moved in here the week after our date."

"Actually, he moved in that same night."

She throws her hands up in the air. "See?"

I laugh.

"But listen, what happens with Emerson's fostering and whatnot?"

I fill her in.

"He's perfect," she says. "Did you know that stupid Corey's still fuming? That boy can't handle anyone taking your time but him, and he's jealous about a kid with no mom."

"Corey's a good person," I say. "He's just—"

"A rich, selfish, controlling brat?"

I sigh. "He's used to getting his own way."

"That too," Barbara says. "But Dave's better looking, and even if he's not rich—"

"He has money," I say. "But like me, it's tied up in this inn."

191

"You best hope this thing does well," Barbara says. "Usually boyfriends are good as a safety net."

"But yeah, if this inn thing bombs, we both fall flat."

"You said it," Barbara says.

"Actually, that's what I'm worried about most."

"It's going to do fine."

"No." I shake my head. "I mean, what I'm worried about with dating him is that if it goes poorly, if we break up. . ."

"Then you're dealing with drama at work, with Emerson, and in your love life."

"It's a lot of places to have drama," I say.

"But it's worth the risk." Barbara nods. "That's always how it goes when you commit to someone. Risks on all fronts."

"How do you know he's worth the risk?"

"I guess I don't, but the fact that you want to date him tells me. You're not the kind of person who wants to date everyone."

"No?"

"You tried to set him up with me—the hot guy who rolled in and paid off your two-million-dollar mortgage."

"Yeah, but only because I knew dating him was a bad idea."

"And then you worked with him and lived with him for weeks and weeks without dating."

"Still."

Barbara hands me my paper carton of rice. "You're just afraid."

"Of?"

"The last time you loved someone as much as you love him, he died."

Best friend, not pulling any punches. "Love's a pretty strong word."

"It fits," Barbara says.

Maybe. Maybe not. I mean, our kiss was electric. Our interactions are always thoughtful.

I think about Dave's actions around me for the last two months. Helping out around the house. Mending and repairing the furniture for my carriage house as often as the furniture for the main house. Cleaning. Helping cook—badly—watching television at night. Standing against the wall with a confident look on his face when his sister called me his girlfriend.

"I think we're more than friends," I admit. "But love is a big word."

"That boy loves you too, you idiot." Barbara practically shoves the paper carton of stir fry at me.

It's hard for me to focus on the show we watch—something with Henry Cavill on Barbara's insistence, and I realize she's right. He does look just like Dave.

Which only makes it harder for me to think about a movie.

After it finally ends and Barbara leaves, I look around for my phone to text Dave. It's sitting on top of the paperwork I'm filling out again, now that Dave and I will both be applying to foster Emerson.

We were almost done, but the last line's about *our relationship*, me and Dave.

There are several boxes and an empty line. One says "married," and that's clearly not us. But the others say "friend" and "committed relationship." My pencil's hovering back and forth between them, and I'm not sure which to check. I finally check friend, but then I have second thoughts and erase it.

Of course, you can still see where I checked it and then erased it. Ugh.

And that's when Dave walks in the door.

"Oh." I drop the pencil. "I was about to text you and tell you she's gone."

His grin's a little sheepish. "I was sitting out in my car. Turns out, Bernie and Bentley are both on dates."

"I'm so sorry," I say. "You should've come back."

"That would have spoiled everything." He walks toward me slowly.

"Like what?"

He drops onto the edge of the table across from me. "Isn't the whole point of girls' nights to dissect every romantic interaction you've had that week and figure out what they mean?"

I straighten up, my eyes flashing. "Excuse me, but it's not the nineteen hundreds any more. We're all feminists now, and not everything we do or say revolves around boys."

"So, yes?" He grins.

I roll my eyes. "Maybe."

"And what did Barbara think?"

"She thinks I'm lucky." I bite my lip.

"That makes two of us." Dave's head lowers toward mine, but right before he kisses me, his eyes widen. His entire head turns sideways. "What's that?"

I follow his line of sight. "Oh. The form."

"I thought we finished it."

I close my eyes. "Well, all but the last question."

"You didn't answer it?"

I open my eyes. "Not yet."

He reaches around me to grab the pencil and swivels around, plopping down on the sofa next to me so he can reach the end table. "The answer's obvious."

"It is?"

"Isn't it?" He lifts his eyebrows. "I mean." His eyes drop to my mouth and he smiles.

"I guess."

He checks the box that says *committed relationship* and drops the pencil. And then he gathers me up in his arms, and he kisses me. And he doesn't stop.

❧ 15 ❧

DAVE

It's a horrible scramble, and we pay a lot in 'expedite shipping' fees, but we manage to change the name of the inn to the Serendipity Inn, and change the logo to Seren's profile.

"I still think we should've used a rabbit's foot," I tease.

Seren's cute nose crinkles. "The dead foot of a precious creature should never have been associated with good luck."

"Still," I say. "People recognize it."

She rolls her eyes. Seren's been able to spot my strange jokes from the start. I think about that first day we spent together, when I made a joke about her horrible tragedy. . .and she laughed.

I should've known right then that she *got* me.

But the thing that really makes our opening a success is the Instagram influencers we manage to book—starting with the somewhat irritating SheShootsSheScores Klara, and ending with a guy who's usually famous for staying in haunted hotels.

Not a Ghost in Sight, but a Vision of her Grandmother was his heading. And that post really took off.

"We're booked out for the better part of the next six weeks." I set the phone down.

Our clerk's an idiot, spending more time filing and painting his nails than making sure the paperwork's in order, but he does show up for work every day.

"And people are loving the gardens." Seren can't hide her smirk.

"It's still summer," I say. "Wait until the fall and see what people think about the vast expanse of dead lawn, and then in the winter, all the mounds of snow, piled up everywhere."

"We'll do ice sculptures and make it an event."

That's why I love her. She ignores my complaining and turns my bad ideas into good ones. "Come here." I hug her and spin her around. "We survived the launch, and we're almost through the first week."

I'm halfway through a decent kiss when her phone rings.

I groan.

But she takes it. Seren's unfailingly responsible. I suppose one of us should be.

"Hello?"

"Mrs. Colburn?"

She clears her throat. She always does that when she thinks it's something important. "Yes?"

"This is Alice Keys." I can barely hear her, but I keep straining.

"Oh, okay."

"I'm Emerson Duplessis's caseworker."

"Right," Seren says. "I remember."

"You've been approved as foster placements for him, you and someone named David Fansee?"

"That's me," I say.

"He's there too?" she asks.

"He is," Seren says. "What do you need?"

"He's been approved for release four days early, and I was wondering whether you could pick him up. You'll be hearing from another caseworker soon, but I wanted to call you since we've met. I have to say, I'm impressed. Very few grand-gesture people, that's what I call people who feel suddenly inspired to become involved, really stick with it."

"Oh." Seren's eyes bulge. "Well, uh thanks." She starts to shake. "Um, so, where do I go?"

"I'll send you an email shortly, and it'll have an address. You'll need to be aware that he may be tired, stressed, or short with you today. Staying in juvenile detention isn't a very relaxing experience."

"Of course."

"But make sure you establish the rules of your house first thing, and show him you mean to enforce them."

Right. The training made it sound like showing them we're the boss was the most important thing.

The next hour or so is a bit of a scramble as my girlfriend loses her ever-loving mind. "A bottle of water." She's searching the room like a detective trying to crack a murder case. "I should have water."

"In the fridge," I say.

"Right."

"But there's already water in the bag you packed." It's a little bit amusing. "My dog had puppies once, you know."

Seren rounds on me, her hands on her hips, her eyes intent. "Are you kidding me right now? What does that have to do with anything?"

"Before she had them, she kept pacing back and forth." I stand up and hand her the bag she packed last week. "Then she'd stop every so often and dig and dig on the carpet. Then she'd go back to pacing. My mom said it was called 'nesting' and that she was trying to make a safe place for her puppies."

Seren's eyes flash. "Now I get it. You're saying I'm like that dog, and that I'm freaking out."

I reach my arms out slowly, letting her have space to back away if she's still upset. But she doesn't. Her nostrils flare, and her eyebrows arch, but she lets me hug her.

And then she collapses against me. "I'm worried. Now that it's finally time, what if that sweet kid I met at the hardware store's gone? What if juvie changed him? What if I was just crazy and seeing what I wanted to see?"

"What if you've built this up in your head, and now the kid isn't great, and he doesn't complete you, and he hates us, and he sets our house on fire?"

Seren looks up at me, her eyes horribly wide. "Minus the fire part, yeah. That's what I was thinking. But now that you mention it, the fire thing, too."

I laugh, and then I press a kiss to the side of her mouth. And then to the other side. "You're very smart. And you saw something that day. I mean, all I saw was the back of him, sprinting toward that car, and then the front of him, scowling at the police. But before all that, you saw him. Something about him made you feel connected. Have faith in that."

She nods. "But it's hard."

"It's going to be hard," I say. "But we've taken the training, and we've read all four books you found."

"I've read eight."

"Of course you have."

"We're ready, right?" She nods.

"Of course we aren't," I say. "Nothing can really prepare you for this. Some days we'll hate him, I imagine, and others we'll be asking each other what on earth we signed up for."

"What?"

I hug her tightly. "That's life. And especially with foster kids. But you and I have both had our share of damage, and now we have each other." I press a kiss to her mouth this time. "And before we go pick up that kid, I should tell you something."

"What?" Her eyes widen again.

I can't help chuckling. "It's good, Seren. Something good." I brush my hand against her beautiful mouth. And then I brush back her breathtaking hair to expose her perfectly curved brow. "I love you, Serendipity Colburn. I love your nose. I love your eyes. Your ears. Your cheek. Your jaw. Your hair. Your curves." I can't help my grin.

She slaps my chest.

"I love when you do that." I catch her hand. "And I love how big your heart is. So when this kid does everything he can to make us regret this, we're going to remember why we're doing it. Because we love each other so much that we want to love someone else, too."

A tear rolls down Seren's cheek. "I love you, too. And even though I'm crying, really, I'm happy. It's just hard for me to be happy without being a little sad."

I love her for that, too. "I know."

She hugs me one more time, and then she grabs that bag—and a chilled water bottle—and we head for the pickup in case he has more bags than will fit in either of our small cars.

Emerson's there, in the same clothes I saw him in that day. A ratty t-shirt and faded jeans. "Hey," he says.

Seren, with watery eyes, rushes up and hugs him.

They've been talking on the phone each week, so I knew she felt like she knew him, at least a little, but I didn't expect the kid to react like he does.

He closes his eyes and hugs her back. And when he lets her go, he looks touched. "Thanks for picking me up." He sniffles a little, like he's got a cold, and he acts like he's fine, but from one tough guy to another, I know what's going on.

Nice try, kid.

Seren was right. She did see something. He does care about her, at least a little.

Once we reach the house, which you can see even through the gate, I can't help hearing his inhalation. "Whoa."

"This was my grandmother's house," Seren says. "It's an inn now, and Dave and I co-own it."

"I didn't know you're rich."

"Not exactly," Seren says. "But I used to be."

It's hard to follow the whole thing while watching through the rearview mirror, but it looks like he's thinking about her words carefully. It makes me wonder what she's told him about her past, about her childhood, her family, and her tragedy.

I'm sure she'll tell him all of it when she's ready.

I just hope he doesn't make things harder on her. It'll be really difficult for me to like the little thief, no matter what I said in my pep talk earlier, if he's making things difficult on Seren.

When we get home, Seren makes dinner and Emerson hovers, like he won't be safe if he's not near her. He laughs awkwardly at the jokes she makes. He follows her with his eyes the entire time, like she might disappear if he stops watching her.

It may be the cutest thing I've ever seen. I worry she'll trip over him, like a mother duck, when she changes directions.

"Here," Seren says at dinner, passing him the plate of breadsticks.

"Why are there two different lasagnas?" Emerson asks. "And that one's super tiny."

"I left the meat out of this one," Seren explains.

"Why?" Emerson frowns.

She swallows. "I'm vegetarian, but that doesn't mean I expect you to be."

He nods. "Okay." Then he looks up at her. "But what if I want to be?"

She stares at him. "Do you?"

He shrugs. "I never thought about it before."

She laughs. "We can talk about it later. But for now, the tiny one's for me."

"Fair enough," he says.

Emerson and I manage to clean up all the lasagna, even the bit left over from the tiny one. After dinner's over, I stand. "I'll clean up."

"I can help," Emerson says. "I always did dishes at the group home."

"It's fine," Seren says. "I'll help. I'm sure you have friends to call or something."

He shrugs. "Not really. Plus, I don't have a phone anymore."

"They took your phone?"

"It was a prepaid, and I couldn't pay." He shrugs again. "It's fine."

"I'll get you a phone tomorrow," Seren says. "I'm sorry I didn't know you needed one."

"I don't, really," he says.

"I hear you need them for school now," Seren says. "Plus, I want to be able to reach you."

His smile is small, but it's there.

If things are a little awkward after dinner, well. I should've expected that. When Jonas from the inn calls me over for a housekeeping issue, I almost breathe a sigh of relief.

When I get back, I peek through the glass beside the door.

Emerson's talking, and Seren's laughing.

Instead of walking in, I sit on the chair on the front porch and wait. A half an hour later, I finally barge back through.

"—until, right at the last minute, she stands up, says, 'I think I've heard enough.' And then she just took my hand and walked out."

"Wow, really?" Seren smiles. "Your mom sounds awesome."

"She was." Emerson frowns. "I mean, she didn't always hold down a job so great, but if I had problems at school, she always had my back."

This is more like it. Problems at school. A mom who couldn't keep a job. This is what we've been prepared for. "We'll help you too," I say. "If you have problems."

"Oh, I had straight As." Emerson looks down at his feet. "Before juvie, that is."

Seren puts a hand on his arm. "You'll get caught up."

"You can't make up work you miss for detention," he says. "But it was just the last week of school."

Seren straightens. "Says who?"

"Um, the school district?"

"That's the most ridiculous thing I've ever heard." She stands up. "I'm going to tell them what I think about it."

"It's fine," Emerson says. "I knew already."

Seren frowns. "Still, I've been thinking. Your school's five metro stops and a line transfer from here. I think you should move to a school that's closer to us."

Emerson freezes.

"Unless you don't want to." She's tentative now. "Would you miss your old one?"

He laughs. "Miss it?"

"I know you're moving from junior high to high school, and it's already a big change. You may want to stay with the kids you know."

"Yeah, not so much."

"You won't miss it, then?"

"No." He shakes his head. "Not at all."

"Then should we enroll you tomorrow for the fall?"

He swallows. "If you want to."

"I insist," she says. "Plus, won't it be easier, now that you'll be here?"

I know that look.

He's worried he *won't* be here.

"Until school starts," Emerson says, "I thought maybe I could help out at the inn. Is there something I can do?"

Alarm bells go off in my head. Why's a teenage boy asking for work? "You're only thirteen, though, right?" I ask. "I don't think it's legal to have you working."

He smiles. "I'm not asking to be paid. But if you're getting me a phone and you're giving me a place to stay, I'd like to do something to help. I'm good in the garden."

"Oh, the bearberry," Seren says. "We could plant it right now."

Emerson glances outside. The sun has set.

"Or tomorrow morning," I say. "No huge rush."

"That's true," Seren says. "I have some ideas for places, but it would be better if you saw them during the day."

"The gardens here are huge," Emerson says. "It's amazing, for a place in the city."

"Grandma loved being in the country," Seren says. "The gardens were Grandpa's way of bringing the country to her, since he had work to do in town all the time." Seren smiles. "Although, at the time, Scarsdale was more of a suburb than it is now."

"What did he do, exactly?" Emerson asks. "Your grandpa, I mean."

I want to know too, so I lean closer.

"He owned a company that made paper goods," she says. "But once it started doing well, he used some of that money to invest in movies." She smiles. "And that's how he met Grandmother and caught her eye."

"That's a fun story." Emerson looks from Seren to me and back again. "But you never told me how you two met."

Seren blushes. "Us?" She glances at me, panicked. "What makes you think we're together? Dave has his own room. He always sleeps there. You don't have to worry."

"Worry?" Emerson's face is comical. "Half the kids at my school have pronouns that change from one day to the next, and if I use the wrong one, they get upset. The other half have more piercings than a fish that can't be caught. All of them vape in the bathrooms when they leave with a hall pass. Trust me, you having a boyfriend isn't really on my list of worries."

"Oh." Seren blinks.

"I fell for her in the first moment I saw her," I say. "When I came to look at the estate with a plan to make it into an inn."

"I thought he was a hare-brained idiot for wanting to remodel the old pile of bricks."

"The only thing we've disagreed on since was what to do with the garden," I say.

"But Emerson likes it, so it stays," Seren says. "He's the tie-breaker now."

"Actually," I say. "You wanted it, so it was always going to stay. I thought that was obvious, since it's still here."

"Always give her what she wants," Emerson says. "Or she'll realize how much better she can do and dump you."

"Hush, kid," I say.

"I say what I'm thinking." Emerson smiles. "And right now, that's that I don't mind if you kiss her in front of me."

"I knew I liked you." I cross the room, grab Seren by her shoulders, and lean close. "He's smart, but he's also kind of an idiot. There's no way you could do better than me."

"Actually, your friend Bentley has more money, has a squarer jaw, and I think he works out more than you." She pokes my chest. "Wait. Strike that. He definitely works out more than you."

"Rude."

"But his sense of humor sucks," she whispers. "And for me, that's a deal killer."

I kiss her then, and Emerson whoops. It kind of kills the mood, but it's cute just the same.

I don't hate the kid.

It's a start.

16

SEREN

S ummers have always been my favorite season. It helps that I grew up in New York where winters are pretty brutal and summers are fairly lovely. Even so, the birds, the sunshine, and the flowers would probably win most people over. Having Emerson around to help in the garden only makes things better. For the first week or so, Dave and I watch him like nervous, first-time mothers.

We kept waiting for something bad to happen.

Only, nothing ever did. He didn't test us. He didn't lie. No matter how many times Dave dumped a wad of cash and change on the entry table, not a single penny ever went missing.

And Emerson works hard.

In the garden, helping when the cleaning people are sick, organizing supplies, you name it, and he will do it without complaint.

"He was a good hire," Dave jokes, three weeks into having him with us. "He's consistently doing more work than we spend on his salary."

I shove his arm. "We pay him nothing."

"I'm not sure that's true. He eats like a future line-backer," Dave says, "and his iPhone's nicer than mine."

I roll my eyes. "That just means you need a new one, grandpa."

"But honestly, he's a really good kid."

"Sometimes people just need a decent pot and some extra water and sun," I say.

"Oh, no, she's talking garden, again. This is why I was opposed to it from the start."

I tilt my head. "And you're acting like you're addressing an audience when I'm the only one around."

Dave laughs. "That's why we're perfect for each other." He grabs my waist and pulls me closer. It's become more and more natural as he does it more and more often. "You're an even better call than the kid." He brushes a kiss against my mouth. "All you needed was some sunshine, some water, and a bigger pot. Who knew?"

I roll my eyes.

"Seren?" Emerson's walking toward us from the side door of the inn.

When he sees us together, he inhales and turns around. "Sorry."

"No," I say. "Come on over."

He's shaking his head as he walks back toward the inn. "It's fine. We can talk later."

I shove Dave away. "No, I want to hear what's up." I jog after him.

Dave's jogging along behind me like a sidecar on a motorcycle, a little behind, a little unnatural looking, but well-intentioned.

"I just had an idea, and I thought. . ." Emerson

looks at his shoes, brand new Nikes I bought him on a whim. He hasn't taken them off since.

"What's the idea?"

He's a little like a slow-moving snail that has to be coaxed out of his shell. At the least bit of noise, he disappears back inside.

"I was organizing the front desk, because . . ."

"Because Kenny's a mess?"

Emerson pushes on. "Anyway, I noticed the bookings, and it seems like we book up pretty well on weekends, but during the week, there are usually quite a few open rooms."

"I think that's pretty normal," I say. "At least, from what I've heard. Weekends are just busier."

"Have you thought about dropping your price for the weeknight rooms, maybe a few days before the stay?"

"You mean discounting them?" I cringe a little. Dave and I have gone back and forth on this, but discounting rooms for high-end inns is a slippery slope. You make a bit more revenue, but you also teach people to expect a 'deal.' It undercuts the value of the brand.

"If you did it through an aggregator, like Priceline, you could claim that it's not a discount. That they got the rate by buying the rooms in bulk."

"But then on top of the cut rate, we pay them a fee."

He bobs his head. "I thought you might say that."

A thirteen-year-old kid thought we might say that?

"So here's what I came up with. Remember your grandma's movie, *Late at Night*?"

"Have *you* seen that?" Dave asks.

"When you two are busy and I'm done with my

work, I've been working my way through her stuff," he says. "You have all those old CDs back at the house."

"DVDs?" I ask.

He shrugs. "Sure."

I stifle a laugh. He's such a Gen Z. "I've seen all her films, yes."

"Well, in that one, she gets chosen by that raffle thing?"

"Okay," I say.

"We get a lot of hits on our website, and based on comments, people love the themed rooms. Some people will change the date of their stay to get the room they want. So maybe we could fill some by letting people enter to win a raffle."

He said *our* website. Like he's claiming it's his, too. It distracts me so much that I miss the next thing he says. "I'm sorry, one more time?"

"It's a stupid idea?"

"Can you explain it once more?"

"Well, if people sign up for dates they'd want to come, and enter their names, and hopefully lots are 'flexible,' then we can send them emails telling them they won a raffle and that they get a discounted rate, tying it in with the movie. It works pretty well, because there *isn't* a particular room for that movie, so we could use it for any of them."

I love the idea.

"Then it's not a 'discount' or a coupon," Emerson says, still clearly anxious to sell his idea. "It's a special deal they're being offered that keeps our brand front and center. Plus, we say as part of the deal, they have to share how much they love their stay on social."

"That's a really good idea," Dave says. "You're a

pretty smart kid." He ruffles Emerson's hair. "Glad you're here to help us."

"Speaking of helping," I say. "It's almost time for that wedding party to arrive. Do we have all the flowers prepared?" The stupid florist got sick, and that left me arranging most of the flowers myself.

I'm not great at it, but I'm better than anyone else on staff. And I'm lightyears ahead of Dave and Emerson. Their attempts looked like they were arranged by a blind person. And somehow, the flowers looked like they were in pain.

All the cleaning crews had to do was distribute them to each room, along with the bride and groom's wedding kits. Only the wedding party's staying here, but the ceremony's being held in the garden.

For a hefty fee.

"Kenny says yes." Dave's statement sounds like a question.

"I should go check."

The rest of the weekend flies by like a whirlwind, the wedding ceremony managing to happen right on time, but only after we succeed in solving about four last-minute emergencies.

Oh, and the bride's wearing my push-up bra.

"They're lucky you're the same size," Dave says. "She wasn't very prepared."

I sink into a chair on the edge of the dance floor, my feet throbbing.

"The best news is, the father-of-the-bride was so happy with everything we did that he gave us this." Dave beams and hands me an envelope.

"What's that?" Emerson sits next to me. "A thank you letter?"

He's been a total champ this weekend, even

dancing with the very awkward, very grumpy daughter of the groom. She started out complaining about everything—didn't want her dad remarrying—and wound up all smiles.

Because Emerson's so stinking cute.

"I hope it's money," I say.

Dave shakes his head. "You're so greedy."

"I've worked my hiney off," I say. "If it's not money, we aren't doing any more weddings."

"Open it," Emerson says. "What if it's a ton of money?"

The envelope's not very thick. I rip it open, unwilling to admit it, but hoping he's right. Could it be. . . a thousand? Five?

"It's a check," I say, unfolding it. My hopes soar. A check. . .that's good, right?

A check for. . .one hundred and twenty-five dollars, and a handwritten note. "Thanks for all you did."

"This will barely buy me a new bra," I complain.

Dave's laughing. "Ah, well. At least we have their credit card on file. You can charge the new bra, if she doesn't return yours, to that, and then spend this on whatever you want."

I collapse against the back of the chair. "Remember what I said?"

"Huh?" Dave's brow furrows.

"The worst thing about life is unmet expectations." I crumple the check and stuff it in my pocket. "I might have been happy for a hundred and twenty-five dollar tip. . .if I hadn't gotten my greedy hopes up." I laugh at myself. "Oh, well."

"Maybe this will cheer you up." Dave drops down on one knee.

And I wonder what fell on the floor. I sit forward, looking around.

"Sit back, woman," he says.

"Oh." Emerson's mouth makes an o, and he sits up straight. "Should I head back to my room?"

"No, you stay." Dave points. "And you." He touches my forehead with one finger and pushes me backward until I'm sitting upright in the chair.

"I wanted to take you to a nice dinner and bring out flowers and really wow you. But that's not the kind of proposal you'd want."

Proposal?

I can barely breathe.

"I thought long and hard about what matters to you. You love your family home, and by extension, our inn. You love gatherings, and seeing people you love. So I thought, hey, after spending the weekend at a wedding, if she doesn't look too shell-shocked. . ."

Barbara pokes her head around the corner. "Hey, there. Is this the right time?"

Dave bobs his head up and down. "Yes. Sit."

She takes a seat to the left of Emerson. "Awesome." She throws me a thumbs up and whips out her phone to film us, I assume.

"So here I am, with a potted bearberry." He drags it out from under a neighboring seat. "And a ring." He pulls that out of his pocket. It's a really big diamond. "And a question." He looks at me, and then he swings around and looks at Emerson, too. "Not just for Seren. For both of you."

Emerson frowns.

"I'd like to ask you, Seren, to be my wife." Dave beams.

"Oh." A whole wave of emotions crashes over me, but the strongest one is definitely joy.

"And I'd like to ask you to be my son." Dave pushes the plant toward him. "This worked for Seren, so I figured I'd try. We can plant it together?"

"Yes," I say. "I'll marry you."

"And what about you, kid?"

"Me?" Emerson says. "I mean, I know New York's progressive, but I don't think I should marry you."

Dave rolls his eyes. "How about it? Wanna be adopted by a shiny newly-married couple?"

"Well." Emerson looks from the bearberry, to the ring, to me, and then back at Dave. "I hate to ruin your plans, but no. I'd rather not."

17

DAVE

M y parents, like any good parents without much education, but who want more for their kids, enrolled me in an SAT prep course. They then drove me to the classes that were nearly half an hour away, three times a week, for nearly a month.

Imagine their disappointment, and my chagrin, when I bombed the SAT.

I mean, lots of kids did worse than I did, but based on my GPA, I should've gotten *way* better than I did. All their hopes of me going to Columbia, or Harvard, or anywhere really prestigious, just *poof*. Gone.

Now I know a little bit about how they felt.

"No?" I blink. "Why not?"

"Hey," Seren says. "I said yes."

"And wahoo," Barbara says. "Most of us are really excited."

"Just not the groom."

It never occurred to me that he'd say no.

"It's nothing personal," Emerson says. "I like you both a lot."

"You *like us*?" Seren swallows. "Oh."

"I love you, even." Emerson puts a hand on hers. "It's just that. . ."

"That what?" I'm still holding Seren's ring. I feel a bit idiotic now about my grand gesture. What's Seren going to think when she looks back on this moment? I thought we'd all look back and think about how our family got started. I had these visions that, thanks to Barbara's help, we'd look back on the video and smile at the moment our family officially began.

I might have even imagined it would go viral on social media.

Because I'm an idiot.

Kind, sweet, smart, hard-working Emerson. . .doesn't want us. And now Seren's going to remember that forever. The night I proposed. . . and the son she wanted rejected us.

Seren stands up. "David Fansee, I'm delighted to marry you."

I'm still down on one knee, trying to catch up.

She grabs my arm and yanks me up to standing. "This is where you swing me around and kiss me," she whispers.

So I do it. I grab her tiny waist, and I swing her around, and I lean down and kiss her, full on the mouth.

"Perfect," Barbara waves.

"But it's not perfect," I say. "Because Emerson said no."

Seren shrugs. "Emerson's a big boy, and I'm sure he has his reasons. But my answer's yes. Isn't that enough to make you smile?"

I shouldn't be surprised that Seren's the one saving

217

the night for us. "Yes," I say. "It is." I can't help my smile then.

"But why did you say no, kid?" Barbara asks. "They're the cutest couple I've ever seen. I'm older than her, and I want her to be my mom."

Emerson glances up at me and Dave. "I really like them. The thing is, though, I have a mom. She died, but not that long ago." He shrugs. "I don't know. It feels. . .disloyal, somehow."

"I think she'd be happy for you to find new parents," Barbara says.

Emerson laughs. "You didn't know her. She's probably swearing up a storm up in heaven, or wherever she is, and pointing. There's no way she wants me to replace her."

"Oh." Barbara sits back in her chair.

"Plus, there are other reasons," Emerson says.

"Reasons?" I sit down, curious now. "What other reasons?"

"Do we annoy you?" Seren asks. "I thought you liked it here."

"It's because I trust you," Emerson says. "Usually kids want to be adopted so they don't have to worry that their new parents will kick them out." He smiles. "I know you won't."

"Uh." I'm still lost.

"And there are lots of grants for foster kids," Emerson says. "Some of them I can get whether I'm adopted or not, but some of them are only for kids who didn't find formal homes. If I know you're keeping me either way, I'd be better off making sure I'll be eligible for everything."

"Grants?" Seren looks flummoxed.

"Plus you'll keep getting a check every month, as long as you're fostering me," Emerson says.

I object this time. "But we don't need—"

"If you don't need it," Emerson says, "then you can put that money into a savings account for me. You can give it to me when I graduate."

"You're a little hyper-obsessed with college, kid," Barbara says.

"You might worry about the future too, if yours had just disappeared." Emerson stands up. "I'm really, really happy for you two. I'm excited for the wedding, and I hope you'll have it here." He smiles. "I'd also like to plant this bearberry with you."

"Okay," I say.

"But I'd rather not be adopted, if that's alright."

"It's fine," Seren says. "Whatever you want."

Emerson drops to one knee this time. "You have no idea how shocked I was when we met that day at the store, and then you stood up for me." He swallows slowly, his eyes intent on hers. "No one has ever stood up for me like that. . .other than my mom."

She lifts one hand and brushes his hair back from his face.

"I really love you, you know. I do." He smiles. "So how about this? I trust you to keep loving me, and you trust me to be your son, even if it's not official on paper?"

Seren's eyes are all watery when she nods.

And then Emerson hugs her.

Barbara may not have caught it on camera, and it may not be the scene I imagined, but it's pretty perfect anyway. For the first time ever, my sweet Seren looks entirely whole.

Emerson insists on sticking around to help the cleaning crew, and Barbara heads home. On our way back to the carriage house, Seren stops me.

She sits on a bench in the garden next to the bearberry she and Emerson planted. I wonder if she realizes where she stopped.

"You proposed tonight."

I realize I'm still holding the ring in my pocket. I whip it out. "I did."

"You have an enormous ring." She looks at it.

I nod. "When I told Mom what I was planning, she insisted I take her ring. If you hate it though, I can give it back and you can pick one."

"Your *mom's* ring?" Seren inhales. "Dave, you are the kindest, the most generous man. But I know you only proposed to try and make us a family. I'm sure it's confusing to explain to your family and friends what we're doing."

"No," I say. "It's not that."

Her smile's understanding. "It's fine. I'm not mad. If I had any family, or friends other than Barbara and Corey—who's still not speaking to me—I'd probably be just as frustrated."

"I'm not frustrated," I say.

"But Dave." She traces my eyebrows, and then her fingers drop to my cheek. "Emerson isn't going anywhere, and neither am I. We don't have to adopt him to prove we care, and you don't have to marry me, either. We'll be just fine without stealing your mom's wedding ring and marching down the aisle."

I sit on the iron bench and yank her down on my lap. "Seren Colburn, when you met me, you told me you were the most unlucky person in the world."

She opens her mouth.

I press a finger to it. "That may have been true. But you transformed my life, and I can't even imagine not having you in it. I really like Emerson—I might even love him. But you, I definitely love. I adore. I dream about you. I think about you morning, noon, and night." I take her hand and slide my mom's ring on her pointer finger. "This ring is way too big—I didn't bother sizing it, because I wanted to see if you liked it first." It's a huge, sparkly, oval-shaped diamond.

"It's beautiful." Seren looks at it, turning it in the moonlight.

"It's not even her engagement ring. That's a tiny stone. Dad was just a trash guy, then. He didn't buy the landfill and start making real money for a long time. When they'd been married twenty years, he bought her that. He said that he loved her at the start, but he loved her more now."

"That's pretty sweet."

"But at the end of the day, my parents are not well-educated." I sigh. "They're loud, they're big-hearted, and they're trash people, through and through."

"Dave."

"Wait," I say. "Because I was called 'garbage guy' for all of college. Not by my friends, but by everyone else. That's who you're dating; that's who your boyfriend is. The garbage guy."

"Dave."

"Still not done." I smile. "It took me a lot of courage to take that ring from my mother—who adores you—and ask you if you'd marry the garbage guy, and join the garbage family. You're blue-blood incarnate. Your grandmother, your grandfather." I wave my hands around. "This house. None of it is Fansee family material."

"Oh, I think it's pretty fancy."

We both laugh.

"You know what I mean," I say. "And if, like Emerson, you'd rather honor the memory of your family by just being with me, then I won't push."

"I love you," Seren says. "I love your handsome face." She traces my eyebrows again. Then her fingers trail down my nose. "I love your generosity, your understanding, and your thoughtfulness." She smiles. "Most of all, I love your willingness to change your mind, to learn, to grow, and to roll with things. Because life with me may be bumpy. I'm not fancy." She sighs slowly. "I'm broken, Dave, and I always will be. No amount of glue or paint or nails can really fix my damage."

"You're beautiful," I say.

"Because you see the beauty in the cracks and the wrinkles." Seren smiles. "That's why I said yes. I don't care about the ring. I don't care about the ceremony. I just care about the promise." She leans closer, placing her head against my chest. "Promise me that, good luck or bad, happy days or miserable nights, you'll stay with me."

"I will."

"Then yes." She sits up again, lifts the ring in the air, and looks at it. "David Fansee, I will be your wife, and I will wear this enormous rock."

"The wife of the garbage guy?" I lift my eyebrows. "Are you sure?"

"No one else I'd rather be." She looks off at the moon. "Did I ever tell you my favorite character on television as a kid?"

I shake my head.

"No one else liked him, but I did. I was obsessed."

"Who?" I ask.

"His name was Oscar," she says. "Oscar the Grouch." She smiles. "And he lived in a silver trash can."

18

SEREN

Dave thought I was kidding when I said I had no family to invite to the wedding.

My grandfather was an only child. So was my dad. My mom had a sister, but she smoked like a chimney and died of lung cancer at age forty-seven. My sister and brother and dad and mom and grandmother all passed in the great tragedy.

Because I didn't send them an invitation (it seemed a little tone deaf) I didn't expect my former in-laws to show up.

They do anyway, and they congratulate me warmly.

Corey comes too, even though he's made it pretty clear that he's not a fan of Dave or the changes I've made since meeting him. On the morning of our wedding, everyone's waiting in their nicest clothes. They all smile and wish me well. Movies and television would have you believe that most humans aren't decent people.

In my experience, the movies are wrong as often as they're right.

Sure, sometimes outrageous things happen.

Tragedy does strike. Sometimes people surprise you with their pettiness and their mean-spirited behavior. But the vast majority of people are just like me.

Trying to make it, one day at a time.

"You look even more beautiful than at your first wedding," my mother-in-law says. Her smile's bittersweet, which is exactly how I feel, thinking about Will. Unlike Emerson's mother, I think Will's up in heaven, smiling down on me. He was always happy for other people's joy.

I think more than anyone else, he'd be happy for mine.

This is the first morning since the accident that I've woken up happy without feeling guilty for it. Because today's my wedding day. The happiest day of my life.

Again.

I should enjoy it. I think my parents would want me to enjoy it, too. I'm standing in front of the mirror, turning to and fro, hoping that the dress Barbara and I chose is tasteful and not too much.

"It's white. I hope that's not tacky," I say. "For a second wedding."

I'm talking to myself, of course, since Barbara already ducked out to let them know I'm ready to walk down the aisle.

That's why I'm so surprised when someone says, "It's not tacky at all."

It's Dave's mother. His loud, big-hearted mother. "You look like you walked right off a set in Hollywood. Or wait." She beams, tears unshed in her eyes. "No. You look like you're just leaving the Buckingham Palace. You could be a real, honest-to-goodness princess."

I smile, then. She's all the things Dave hates about his family. She's in-your-face, she's larger-than-life, and she's unapologetically opinionated.

She's all the things I wish I was.

And I love her for it, almost as much as I love Dave. "Thank you," I say. "I know the wedding was expensive, and Dave and I have all our money sunk in this inn."

"You provided the venue," Mrs. Fansee says. "That's more than enough."

"But usually the bride's family—"

Mrs. Fansee can really move, for a large woman. She crosses the room in a split second and wraps me in her ample arms. "We're your family now," she says. "And I couldn't have picked a better daughter-in-law if I tried."

The tears that have been threatening finally fall, and I know my makeup's probably running down my cheeks. I can't even form words. What would I say? That I'm grateful? That they're lovely? That people don't usually get a second chance to have a family? That as much as it hurt to lose the family I loved with all my heart, somehow, them embracing me like their own has healed all my jagged, torn edges?

It's all true.

I can't say any of it.

But the way Mrs. Fansee wipes my tears and squeezes my cheeks makes me think she already knows.

"You've made my standoffish, insecure, snobby son happier than I ever thought he'd be. He told me, you know, about how you can't have kids, and how you thought that made you not good enough." Mrs. Fansee sighs. "I've wanted to say something for a long while, but I wasn't rightly sure what to say."

"I'm sure it's disappointing," I say.

She shakes her head. Her entire face turns red, and her cheeks start to tremble. "Not at all. If you knew how stupid I felt." She starts to cry in earnest then. "You are such an angel, and all my stupid talk at that shower must've made you sad. I'm just so sorry."

I inhale deeply, and shake her. "You didn't make me sad."

She cuts off, wiping her eyes. "What?"

"I wasn't sure, then, how to mourn my daughter." I look up at the ceiling to try and keep from crying again. "It's hard, even now, to think about her. But it's healing too, thinking about the things that cause us pain. And that shower helped me start to heal. I'm really sad that I can't have children, but—"

"But you're doing something even more brave, something we're all just tickled pink about."

I blink.

"You're taking in children who need you more than anyone." She's crying again. "Children that not everyone knows how to love."

"Do you mean Emerson?"

She nods. "Dave's pa and me are so proud of you for taking him in." She beams. "He's just the brightest boy, and you all three shine like stars."

"Thank you." Dave's mother may have embarrassed him in the past, but I've rarely met someone who's quite so accomplished at loving people. It's a rarely acknowledged skill, and it's probably a mother's most important attribute.

"Listen, I also came by, because someone had a favor to ask."

"A favor?"

A man clears his throat near the doorway, and I spin around to see who it is.

Dave's father, Mr. Fansee, is wearing a tuxedo that's a little too small, but no one will notice, thanks to the big grin on his face. "I'm just a trash guy," he says. "But my finest hour, my most wonderful day, was the day I walked my little girl, Danika, down the aisle."

Danika's here today, with her one-month-old baby girl and toddler son. I felt a little bad, planning it so close to her baby's birth, but she told me it's perfect. She said it gave her the perfect excuse to be a little "fluffier" than she'd like to be.

Dave's dad's beaming, his white hair carefully combed, with just a little tuft of it still sticking up in the back. "I'd be honored if you'd let me walk you down that aisle today."

Because I don't have anyone else to do it.

He's telling me it's for him, but I know the truth. He's here for me. To try and make sure that I'm not alone on that walk. "Truth be told, Dave sent me. He said he'll walk with you the rest of your life, but this one time, could I make sure his girl's smiling when she comes down the aisle?"

I nod, wiping at my eyes one more time.

"Weddings is supposed to be happy," Mrs. Fansee says. "So you two stop weeping and sobbing and get out there." She's wiping her own eyes as she says it.

"Are they ready for me?"

"Girl, my son's been waiting his whole life for you," Mr. Fansee says. "But in this case, he's been tapping his foot for at least twenty minutes."

I laugh. That sounds like Dave.

"Once he makes up his mind, he wants it done yesterday," Mrs. Fansee says. "I hope you're ready for that."

But when we walk out the door of my dressing room, someone else is waiting. Emerson's wearing the brand new suit I just bought him, and he has never looked more uncomfortable in the entire time I've known him.

Including when he was standing in front of the cops after stealing that drill.

"Is everything okay?" I ask.

"Can we talk for a minute?" He looks behind me at the Fansees.

"We'll wait," Mrs. Fansee says. "Go ahead."

"I know Dave's getting antsy," I say.

Mr. Fansee rolls his eyes. "We'll tell him to hold his horses." He waves his hand. "Go."

Emerson and I step back into the room and close the door. "Is everything alright?"

Emerson nods, but he doesn't look very sure.

"If you're—"

"You never asked me why I stole that stuff," Emerson says. "I kept thinking you would, but you never did."

"Oh." That's not what I expected him to say. "Well, you didn't offer it, and I didn't figure it would help to pressure you about it."

"It's just that, I want today to be a happy day, but." He swallows. "It's also the day my mom died."

"Oh." I blink. "I'm—I'm so sorry."

"I was helping that terrible lady—she was a cafeteria worker at my school—steal that stuff, because she said she'd give me half the money if I did. I needed money to buy a marker for Mom's grave. They said

229

they'd make one, but they never did. Her grave's just a number in the government plot out there, down bus route fifty-nine."

"I—I wish I'd known," I say. "I never would have picked today for the wedding."

He looks up then. "It's not that," he says. "I think it's good to have something happy today. It's just that, I keep thinking about how you and Dave are like my mom and dad now. I never had a dad, but I loved my mom, and I know she'd hate for me to replace her. And I haven't even been a good son. She died two years ago, and I still haven't gotten her a marker for her grave." He looks sick.

"We can buy one," I say. "I'd be happy to—"

He shakes his head. "I need to earn it. But could you maybe pay me for extra work around the inn, or something? Then I could use the money I earned to buy her grave marker?"

"Sure," I say. "I'd be happy to do that."

He nods. "Okay. And I'm sorry for wrecking your wedding." He winces. "Really sorry."

I cup his cheek. "Emerson, you never asked me something, either."

"What?"

"You never asked why I wanted to be your foster mom."

He frowns. "You didn't offer, and I didn't want to pressure you." His sly grin tells me he knows he's copying me.

"A little over a year and a half ago, now, I was pregnant, on a vacation with my parents, my grandmother, my siblings, and my husband."

"I know." Emerson shrugs. "I looked it up."

I nod. "I should've told you that before, but it

seemed like a dark rain cloud, and you have enough of those."

"It's why you know how it feels to be sad." He forces a smile. "It's why you get me."

"Probably true," I say. "But I didn't tell you and it's not in the news that I was pregnant that day." I hiccup. "I lost the baby, and I also lost my uterus in a surgery afterward. It's how they stopped the bleeding and saved my life. But it means I can never have any children of my own."

"Oh." His brow furrows. "I'm sorry."

"For over a year, I felt pretty sorry for myself. I'd always wanted to be a mother, in the same way some women wanted to be ballerinas, or movie stars, or singers. I spent my nights thinking about how, one day, I'd have a family all around me. I'd host large family dinners. I'd make cakes for birthdays and anniversaries, and for holidays, we'd barbecue."

"Portobello mushrooms, maybe." Emerson smirks. He's been vegetarian since the second day he joined us. It makes him the first person in my life to ever change his eating habits for me. "It sounds nice. I'm sorry."

"When I met you, it was like landing the leading role in a movie. If that didn't sound worse than losing a finger to me."

"Lovely."

"When I met you, I saw that family in my future again, just a little different than before. I realized that, as broken as I was, there were other people like me. People who weren't always lucky, people who had been hurt, and people who were sad and maybe still hurting. But like me, they were also people who wanted love. Maybe even people who *needed my* love. That's why from that day on, I saw you and thought of my future family."

Emerson's crying now, too.

"I seem to be making everyone cry."

"I hear tears are good luck for weddings," he says.

"We better go out," I say. "How raccoon-y do my eyes look?"

Emerson laughs. "You look perfect, as always."

"Let's go."

Mr. and Mrs. Fansee are waiting, and Dave's dad holds out his arm, but Emerson waves him off. "I thought maybe I could walk Mom down the aisle?"

It's the first time he's ever called me 'Mom.' I hope it doesn't make his real mother angry.

I'm crying too much to say anything, but I nod. Dave's parents seem to get it. They follow us out. At least they know why I'm crying as I walk down the aisle toward my new life. Dave knows me well enough to chuckle as he sees me coming.

He raises his voice so everyone can hear him. "Listen folks, the bride's crying, but I swear, it's not my fault."

Everyone turns toward him, and the people who know him start to laugh. Which is most everyone, since almost none of the guests are people I invited.

"Alright, Father, let's get this started."

"I'm not a father," the reverend says.

"Whatever," Dave says.

We're lucky Reverend Andrews agreed to marry us. My future husband believes in God, but he's as close to a heathen as someone who believes can be.

The ceremony's beautiful, and the weather's perfect. The audience listens, and even Danika's baby stays quiet as a mouse.

"The bride told me you won't be exchanging vows," Reverend Andrews says.

"But I do have a little something to say. Is that alright?" Dave asks. "This is where I tell her what I'm promising, in addition to the normal sickness and health stuff?"

Reverend Andrews looks confused.

"Great." Dave plows on. "So here's what I wanted to say. I've been worried my entire life that deep down, like all the kids at school said, I was just a garbage guy. I thought I didn't really belong at the smart school or in the refined social circles."

"You're the best," one of his friends shouts.

Lots of others laugh.

"When I met Seren, I knew I wasn't good enough for her. Compared to her, whatever I was before, I was definitely a garbage guy. But I remember one thing from economics class back in school. Buy low, sell high. So that's what I did. When she was feeling a little blue, I was there, smiling. And believe it or not, it worked. This staggering woman agreed to marry me —me! And here we are. I'm still the happiest man in the world, and I discovered something."

He leans close to me and presses a kiss to my forehead. Then he pulls something out of his pocket, licks it, and sticks it to my cheek.

"I may be a garbage guy, but with her at my side, people think we're movie stars. Ladies and gentlemen, if you marry a superstar, it doesn't matter what kind of man you are. You rise to her level. So my promise to you, Seren, is that, every day of the rest of my life, I'll try to stay on your level. I'll try to be the kind of man you deserve. A rockstar guy. Not a trash man."

He brushes one hand against my face gently.

233

"And I'll try to love you just as much if not more than I loved you that first day we met. . .every single day of our lives." He leans in close and *nips* at my face. I realize he's eating a Cheerio.

That punk.

His parents start to clap and cheer, and his sister whoops so loudly it wakes her baby.

"Looks like my garbage family approves," Dave says.

Now everyone's laughing.

"I said we didn't want to exchange vows," I say, "because I'm not good in front of people." I turn away from the sea of people I don't know, and I look just at Dave. "But I can't say *nothing*, not after all that."

The people I'm trying to ignore cheer. It makes them hard to ignore.

"I guess I wanted to say that when Dave and I met, I felt really unlucky. I had felt that way most of my life, to be honest. But when I met Dave, that all changed. I thought at first that maybe he was my good luck charm."

I feel like this may be something that other people need to know. So I force myself to turn toward the audience.

"Maybe he is my good luck charm." I sigh. "Or maybe I was looking at it all wrong. The world's full of all kinds of luck, things we can't explain, and things we can't control. You can be both lucky and unlucky, sometimes in the same day. But if you're intelligent enough to look for it, you can always see the good luck alongside the bad. And I believe that God will send you joy to counteract the pain, if you keep hoping and believing through all the misery."

I look back at Emerson.

"Sometimes we lose things—things we think we can't bear. But later on, we'll find other sources of joy. I found a son I hadn't given birth to, and I found a husband I don't really deserve. And I'm happier than anyone has a right to be." I smile. "So if you feel like your luck is down, or that your month has been a mess, brace yourself. The good news is probably right around the corner. Be smart enough to see it."

I turn back toward Dave.

"My promise to you is that I won't be a little storm cloud. I'll look for the light shining through, and you and I, together, no matter what luck comes, will smile. Because we've gotten really good at smiling together, even when things go wrong. I feel like, for people who also work together, that's about the best promise I can make."

After that, the reverend tells us we can kiss, and boy does Dave take it literally. Eventually, even the crowd gets annoyed.

"Alright, son," Reverend Andrews says. "That's enough."

Dave finally releases me, and he shrugs. "Look at her. Can you blame me?"

Everyone finds him almost as charming as I do. Maybe that's the biggest difference between Dave and Will. Will was kind to everyone, and Dave makes everyone laugh. Their differences are what allow me to love Dave without guilt. Because he's not like Will, but he's just what I need now, after losing Will.

A breath of sunlight and breeze.

Laughter in the face of misery.

Dave took me all broken down and sad and he fixed me. The reception feels almost superfluous after all that. But we do all the things anyway. We cut a cake, we dance, and we chat with all the guests. I even throw my flower bouquet, which fittingly has bearberries in it.

Barbara catches it.

I'm yawning, which is my sign that we're about done, when Emerson finds me again. "Hey, sweetheart. I hope you're having fun."

He nods. "I just wanted to tell you something. I've been thinking about it all night."

"Okay."

Dave grabs my arm, but I shake him off. "Gimme just a minute."

He nods and turns away to chat with his dad.

"You told me about your baby." Emerson frowns. "And I didn't know what to say."

"It's alright." I squeeze his hand. "That happens to me a lot. You don't have to say anything. I know how you feel."

"But I wanted to say this. I'm really sorry you lost her." He stares at me intently. "But I'm also not so upset, because if you hadn't lost her, you might not have wanted me." His bottom lip trembles.

Oh.

"And I'm really glad you want me." He hugs me then, fiercely, his head pressed against my shoulder. "Thanks for, you know. Wanting me."

He hugs me like that, like a barnacle holding on for dear life to the side of a boat, for a few moments.

Eventually, Dave comes back. "Hey, hands off my wife, kid. We've got to go."

Emerson releases me and glares at Dave. "What? Where are you going?"

"I heard you wanted to earn some money," Mr.

Fansee says. He must have followed his son over. "I might've eavesdropped a bit at the door earlier."

Emerson looks horrified.

"Big families." Mr. Fansee shrugs. "Good and bad about being part of one. Some of the good though is that our family's big on earning money. And we got foster certified, so while Dave and Seren go on a honeymoon, you get to come stay with us and learn about the original family business."

"The original. . .?" Emerson glances at me desperately.

"You're going to spend the last week of summer riding on a trash truck, kid," Dave says. "Good chance to build up those puny biceps of yours."

His face is classic.

A moment later, he looks more resolved to the idea. "You said you'll pay me for it? How much?"

"Twelve bucks an hour," Mr. Fansee says. "Best in the city."

"How about fourteen?" Emerson says. "I'm an orphan, didn't you hear?"

Mr. Fansee's roar has the entire room turning toward us. He pats Emerson on the back and says, "This ain't *Annie*, kid, and I'm no Daddy Warbucks. It's more like *Ratatouille*, truth be told, but I'll think about it."

"Rat-a-what?" Emerson asks.

"I know what we're watching tomorrow night," Mr. Fansee says. "After a long day's work, that is."

Emerson looks shell-shocked as we walk away, but I know he's in good hands. Because now the Fansees, and Emerson, and Dave, we're all one big family.

And that's what I needed all along—to belong.

T H E E N D!

*** I hope you loved Seed Money! If so, it would be amazing if you could leave me a review wherever you like to read. The next book in the series, Nouveau Riche, will feature Emerson's love story... I hope you're as excited to read it as I am to write it. You can preorder it now.

ACKNOWLEDGMENTS

My husband makes everything I do possible by his general awesomeness. Sometimes, some people who are WAY TOO COOL to contain their awesomeness in their body just ooze epic-ness everywhere. It's been known to make them lose their hair, but the good news is, it makes them even better looking. I'd like to thank Whitney for being willing to be JUST THAT AWESOME.

My Emmy and my Dora and my Tessa are just the most supportive girlies any mother could have. And my mom is pretty epic with her support and cheerleading as well. The women in my life are the best yes-men I could ask for.

My editor Carrie is unfailingly THERE for me, even when I inconvenience her. Even when she's sick. Even when I think she can't get things done with no notice, she figures it out. LOVE.

And to my readers/fans. I LOVE YOU GUYS SO MUCH. Thank you for loving and supporting my writing. Without you, I'd just be word pollution. KEEP READING, my lovelies. I ADORE YOU.

ABOUT THE AUTHOR

I have animals coming out of my ears. Seven horses. Three dogs, three cats, thirty-ish chickens. I am always doctoring or playing with an animal... and I wouldn't want it any other way. But Leo is still my very favorite.

When I'm not with animals, or even if I am, I'm likely to have at least one of my five kids in tow, two of which I'm currently homeschooling.

I also love to bake, like to cook, and feel amazing when I kickbox and rollerblade. Oh yeah, and I'm a lawyer.

I adore my husband, and I love my God.

The rest is just details.

ALSO BY B. E. BAKER

The Scarsdale Fosters Series:

Seed Money

Nouveau Riche

The Finding Home Series:

Finding Grace (0)

Finding Faith (1)

Finding Cupid (2)

Finding Spring (3)

Finding Liberty (4)

Finding Holly (5)

Finding Home (6)

Finding Balance (7)

Finding Peace (8)

The Finding Home Series Boxset Books 1-3

The Finding Home Series Boxset Books 4-6

The Birch Creek Ranch Series:

The Bequest

The Vow

The Ranch

The Retreat

The Reboot

The Setback

Children's Picture Book

Yuck! What's for Dinner?

I also write contemporary fantasy and end of the world books under Bridget E. Baker.

The Russian Witch's Curse:

My Queendom for a Horse

My Dark Horse Prince

My High Horse Czar

The Magical Misfits Series:

Mates: Minerva (1)

Mates: Xander (2)

The Birthright Series:

Displaced (1)

unForgiven (2)

Disillusioned (3)

misUnderstood (4)

Disavowed (5)

unRepentant (6)

Destroyed (7)

The Birthright Series Collection, Books 1-3

The Anchored Series:

Anchored (1)

Adrift (2)

Awoken (3)

Capsized (4)

The Sins of Our Ancestors Series:

Marked (1)

Suppressed (2)

Redeemed (3)

Renounced (4)

Reclaimed (5) a novella!

A stand alone YA romantic suspense:

Already Gone